DARK MOON

THE GODDESS CHRONICLES

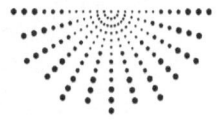

KB ANNE

Published by Gripping Tales, LLC, Pennsylvania.

ISBN: 978-1-956915-02-0

Cover Design by Anika Willmans, Ravenborn Covers

Editorial Services by Laura Parnum, Laura Parnum Books

❀ Created with Vellum

To Destiny,
You didn't know I was wading through the murky waters of
whether I should write YA or write for adults.
Thanks for unsticking me!

JOIN THE KOVEN

Read Clarissa and Carman's origin story, The Druids Sisters of the Gallicennial, FREE by signing up for K's Koven. Be the FIRST to find out about new releases from Best-Selling Author, K.B. Anne. PLUS, receive Newsletter Subscriber Only Bonus Content, insight on Celtic Mythology, Druids, Witches, Werewolves, and Magic, and so much more! Join K's Koven today!

PROLOGUE

"From the beginning comes the end. From the end comes the beginning."
—Sisters of the Order of Brigit.

NEW DRAMA

The fairy mound looks so ordinary from Alaric's thinking rock. There's little indication of the wonders awaiting on the other side of it. The vibrant greens. The brilliant blues. Mom. Gram. Maybe even Dad by now. I might be a reincarnated goddess but that doesn't mean I've been downloaded with all the information I'll ever need to know about the admission process to the Otherworld. In fact, it's the complete opposite. Last night, after the cows plowed Clayone into the depths of my shrine, one of them licked my cheek. With that sandpaper kiss, Brigit's memories were wiped away with it. Leaving just me, Gigi Brennan, a girl who lies. Who cheats. Who steals. A girl of no exceptional worth or value, whose family gave their lives so that she might live.

And if the allure of seeing my family again wasn't enough of a temptation to visit the Otherworld, the faint scent of honey blossoms and the whispers of fairy wings try to trick me into visiting. But I know if I return anytime soon, I'll remain there forever, and I have far too much living to do in this one first. I owe Gram, Mom, and Dad a long, full life, or at least that's what everyone keeps telling me. The jury's still out on that one.

I rub my new crystal necklace back and forth across my lips. Clarissa gave it to me this morning. Most likely as a bribe because she wouldn't let me go with her, Amorin, and a few other coven members when they left for Carman's bonfire to take care of last night's fallen. It's not that I possess some fascination with rotting Maleficium witch corpses, but I wanted proof that Carman was dead and that the entire evening wasn't a result of a grossly overactive imagination. But when I asked Clarissa if I could go, she insisted I stay with Scott while he recovered from his wounds. I tried to argue with her. I might have even added in some I'm-a-goddess-don't-you-want-me-to-be-happy? whining, but she manipulated me into doing exactly what she wanted. She wasn't above using Scott as a deterrent— I admired her approach.

When she gave me the necklace, she told me the crystal along with the ring of amethyst stones would soothe me with their calming properties and alleviate my grief and sadness. I told her a few stones wouldn't fix what's wrong with me. Just because I'm a reincarnated goddess doesn't mean I can't be a bitch too. She gave it to me anyway.

I suppose, in a way, the necklace did help me this morning. It distracted me while they were gone and Scott was sleeping. I studied the crystal and the amethysts in the sunlight, searching for imperfections. I didn't find any. Then I focused my energy into it to see if I could make it glow. I couldn't, but it passed the time. After a few hours, I grew restless and ornery. Amorin sensed as much when he returned from the bonfire site. He suggested I go for a walk and stretch my legs. That's how I ended up at the fairy mound thinking about everyone I lost to a psychotic, oversized werewolf and a power-hungry, revenge-bent witch. Amorin, or Granda—it's still feels weird to call him that when I only recently discovered I had a mom and dad who actually cared about me—alluded to another prophecy, the real reason why Scott and I reincarnated. I can't imagine a fight more devastating and emotionally draining than the one we barely survived last night. With the exception of Scott, everyone I love is dead. How could things get worse?

"Why does my siofra continue to carry such heavy burdens?" Alaric's enchanting baritone voice calls out to me. I turn to face him, and my heart immediately fills with heat. His beautiful, dancing, emerald-green eyes remind me of the Otherworld—vivid and full of life. The moment his lips meet mine, my fears and worries magically disappear. At Metropol all those weeks ago, I blacked out after we kissed. Whether because of the radioactive chemistry between us or because I'd unknowingly taken something, I don't know. But each kiss since then strengthens me. It's like he gives me energy when everyone else seems to take it away.

Too soon, he pulls back, dazzling me with his deliciously mischievous smile and sparkling white teeth.

"I missed you," he whispers, inhaling deeply. "I told you I'd come back to you. I will always come back to you. I will always find you. You believe me, don't you?" he murmurs, his eyes intense.

Content to bask in his attention, I smile back at him. "Uh-huh," I manage to reply, sounding like the dimwit Scott likes to call me and not the goddess I am.

He brushes a lock of my hair behind my ear. "I came straight to you. I didn't even stop at home because I couldn't wait to see you. I have good news."

For some reason chills run down my spine, as if I somehow know that what he's about to tell me is not good news at all. In fact, it's downright terrible news. "Go on," I whisper when he doesn't continue.

"Right before I left, Nan told me my dad was coming home. I want you to meet him. I want you to be a part of my life."

I extract myself from his hold, breaking whatever spell we cast together whenever we touch. I turn away to face the fairy mound. A pit roots in my stomach. There are many things I know about his nan and his "aunt," Calliope, that he doesn't know—or at least I don't think he does. If he knew they wanted me dead, he wouldn't have left me yesterday. He might have been raised by them, he might even be dedicated to them, but I believe with all my being that his feelings for me are stronger. That being said, this new piece could be the surprise Carman warned me about. I hate surprises—especially if they have anything to do with psycho witches of any kind. I'm fickle like that.

"How long has your dad been gone?"

He embraces me from behind, nuzzling my neck. "Fifteen years."

My heart speeds up, my vision blurs, and I suspect I begin to lose the ability to speak, but my next question is much too important not to ask.

"What's your dad's name?"

"Clayone."

The edges of consciousness slip away.

"Gigi? Gigi! Are you okay?"

I find myself cradled in Alaric's arms, his warmth permeating my soul, making me better, stronger, at peace. Making me hate myself more than I already do for being so weak. Screw the damsel-in-distress routine. I need to get my blood sugar checked. I can't pass out every freaking time something shocking happens—especially since something shocking occurs daily. Next time it might not be someone who cares about my well-being catching me.

And I have to believe that Alaric cares about me. Despite who I am. Despite who he is.

"What did you say your father's name was?" I hope beyond reasonable, rational hope that I heard him wrong as a result of someone shoving cotton balls in my ears when I wasn't paying attention.

"Clayone."

Cold certainty wraps around my heart. I shrink into myself and roll out of his grip and into a standing position. I *was* firm in my belief that he cared for me more than he cared for his nan or his "aunt." But this new reveal, this blasted surprise from Carman, could ruin us.

His hands curl around my biceps from behind. For the first time in his presence I realize how very breakable I am. I command myself not to shudder from his touch. My body, however, ignores my warnings.

"Gigi, what's wrong?"

I pull away from him. "I'm not feeling well. I need to go home."

He rushes over to me. "Let me help you. You look terrible."

I drop my eyes. I can't look at him. I want to, but I can't. It's devastating that the one person, the first person I finally feel something for, might be the one most terrible for me. The one whose father wanted to kill me so I imprisoned him for all of eternity instead.

He draws me into a tight embrace. My initial, natural impulse allows me to sink into him. Then my brain reminds me why I can't. Why I shouldn't. I break away and start cutting across the meadow toward Granda's cottage and either a psych evaluation or a straitjacket. I haven't decided which yet, but probably both. "I got it. It's not far."

He easily catches up to me and swings his arms around me as if to carry me. I try to resist, both frustrated that he thinks I can't walk on my own and also that I can't let him. I can't let myself care for him more than I already do. I swat at him, but he completely ignores my effort and sweeps me off my feet.

"Alaric, I'm fine. Let me walk."

He's the only one who has purposely held me when I could actually move by my own power—first at Carman's and now here. Scott, Ryan, and random strangers have carried me when I wasn't completely coherent, but Alaric possesses some impulsive need to cart me around. The quirk endears him to me even more, which given the current circumstances is unfortunate and potentially hazardous to any long-term living goals I might have. My head, with a mind of its own and quite possibly a death wish, rests on his chest.

"Better?" he asks, his voice like a cat's purr.

I tell myself to forget about the potential future drama and conflict that is bound to occur between us and soak in this feeling of security and comfort, because inevitably, in the end, it'll all go to shit. Why should the fact that I now know I'm a goddess be any different?

"Everything all right, Gi?"

He can either read my mind—which I pray to the gods he can't—or he can read my body language, which at least doesn't indicate that a war was waged last night and his family lost. My family lost too, but in a much different way.

I nod, afraid that my voice will betray me. He pulls me in closer, as if sensing I need comfort. Which I do. Maybe he does too.

All too soon our time together comes to end. We wind up at Granda's faster than I would have if I had walked on my own two feet. He lets himself into the front gate with me still cradled in his arms. The gate creaks behind us, but it's not the noise it makes that alarms me—it's my enraged brother stalking down the path.

"Who the hell are you?" he growls.

Alaric's arms tighten. "I can ask you the same."

"I'm her brother. Put her down."

His tension eases, but it still boils just below the surface. "Brother? Gi never mentioned her brother was here."

Scott stops in front of me. "She never mentioned you either. Now, unhand her."

I struggle to lift my head because my brother can't possibly expect I'd let him talk in such a manner.

"Oh my god, Scott. 'Unhand her'? What are you, an Arthurian knight returned from the dead?"

He glares at me. *Quiet.*

I haven't even gotten started yet.

"I said, put her down," he hisses.

I glare at him. "And I said, I'm not done yet."

He scowls at me in return. *You realize you just admitted you can read minds.*

"I've done no such thing." Then I realize I have, but it's too late to cover up my mistake. Who knows...maybe evasion will work. "Alaric, would you mind setting me down now?"

He obliges, which is also surprising. Most people don't listen to me, let alone honor my requests. Well, except for Granda's coven, but only when I act goddess-like, not when I'm just Gigi. I cross my arms and stare at Scott. He can be a downright bastard when he wants to be.

Alaric rests his hands on my shoulders. It makes him seem like he's on my side. That he'll always be on my side, regardless of the secrets I keep from him.

"Scott, Alaric. Alaric, Scott. Now, play nice."

Alaric reaches a hand over to Scott, palm out. Scott scowls at me again before extending his. If he keeps up the constant facial disapproval, he'll get wrinkles deeper than the Grand Canyon. Would serve him right too.

There are firm handshakes and then there are iron death-grip handshakes. I watch as veins and tendons strain and knuckles whiten. Before any bones break, I rest my hands on top of theirs. Their grips soften immediately. At least I retained some of the Goddess Brigit's healing touch, or maybe the crystal and amethysts actually work.

"There, there. Now let's make peace."

Scott rolls his eyes and releases his grasp. "Nice to meet you, Alaric."

"Likewise," Alaric says, returning his hand to my shoulder.

The three of us stand in an awkward testosterone-filled silence.

"Scott, I'd like to speak to Alaric for a minute."

"Sure," he says.

"Why don't you go inside, and I'll meet you in there?"

His arms return to their crossed position. "I'll wait."

I raise my eyebrows. "I'd like to speak to him a-*lone*."

He growls, "Fine," and stomps up the path and into the cottage, leaving the front door open so he can eavesdrop. He's un-freaking-believable.

I turn to face Alaric.

A touch of accusation sparks his pupils. "You didn't mention your brother was here."

I'd like to be as up-front and honest as possible with Alaric because there are already far too many secrets between us. I also don't want to send him home to an empty house—or worse—to the fallen remains of his nan and his aunt in case Granda and Clarissa left them at the bonfire site. But I need to figure some things out. A lot of things. Like is Alaric really Clayone's son? And if so, is he a werewolf? And if so, will he want to kill me too? You know, run-of-the-mill teenage drama.

But I ignore those nagging concerns and reach for his hands to pour good-vibe energy into them. "He just got here yesterday."

"And he already got into a fight. Not surprising, given his bad attitude."

Even without being able to read his mind, I know he means the bruises covering most of Scott's face. Unfortunately, it was much worse than a fight. It was a battle between life and death. But it's the wounds Alaric can't see that are the real cause of worry.

"He's protective of me."

Alaric stiffens. "Did someone mess with you when I was gone?"

I reach up and wrap my hands around his neck to pull his lips to mine. "He's not the only one protective of me."

He smiles before our lips meet.

Quit it. Scott pours all his focus into making me hear his single thought.

Of course, I ignore him.

"Ahem," he clears his throat.

I break away and turn to him. "Really? Privacy, please."

"We need to talk *now*," he says.

"In a minute."

Right now.

"Fine."

Alaric looks from me to the open door where Scott is standing and back to me. "Do you two read each other's minds?"

I pull away from him. I forget myself when we're together. "What? That's weird. No. Just brother-sister ESP."

He dips down in front of me, studying my reaction. "Are

you sure? Because I only heard part of the argument, but it seems decisions were made."

His powers of observation will only add to the trouble.

"Would you mind leaving and maybe meeting at our secret spot later?"

He eases back into me. "And finish what we've been trying to start."

I wink as I step away. "Something like that. Meet at say . . . nine."

"Brilliant. Leave your brother at home."

I glance up at Scott who's been shouting in my head for the past several seconds. "Make it ten, and that shouldn't be a problem."

A little sleeping potion never hurt anyone.

"Until then, sweet Gigi," he says, leaning down for another kiss.

My insides turn to mush, which I never thought would be possible. I assumed my organs were made of granite and vinegar along with a heavy dash of toxic sludge. "Until we meet again," I murmur as our lips find each other once more.

THINK MUCH?

*S*cott stands with arms crossed, scowling at me when I enter the cottage. His eyes are red and puffy from crying—the death of Dad and Calliope still fresh in his mind. But he won't let such a weakness as mourning stop him from being angry at me for bringing home a guy.

I walk right past him on my way to the stove. "What are you staring at?"

Gram's tea will settle my mind. And after the past few days, I need some settling. As for the tea dulling my magic? That is the least of my worries. Ding-dong the witch is dead, the Big Bad Wolf is locked away, and most of my family is dead. I should forget the tea and go for a freaking sedative. Losing a few decades to unconsciousness should help ease the pain.

"Who's the dude?"

I stop and look at him. "Did you just say 'dude'? What is this, 1950?"

He fidgets with Dad's journal. "People say, 'dude.' If I said, 'man' or 'greaser' and broke out into song, then maybe you'd be justified in making fun of me, but 'dude' is perfectly acceptable."

I laugh as I fill the kettle. I missed this mindless, lighthearted banter. When I first arrived to Amorin's, Ireland didn't hold that spark I assumed it would. It wasn't until I met Alaric that I really began to love it. And now, with Scott here, it feels like home. I never thought any place would feel like home again after Gram's death. Now I realize, home is where Scott is.

"What's with the I-art-thou-goddess look?"

I fling a tea bag at him. He catches it with his freakishly fast reflexes and adds it to his mug.

"I do not look goddessy. Aren't I allowed to be happy that my annoying brother has finally joined me after hanging out in prison for weeks?"

He winces. The memories come rushing back to him. The sharp knife of emotion, both his and mine, slices through me and chops me up into itty bitty bite-sized pieces. The pain and sadness he felt killing Ryan. The loneliness at the juvenile detention facility. The confusion when Calliope arrived unexpectedly and freed him, only to imprison him upon landing in Ireland. The hurt and disappointment that the mother he dreamed of loving betrayed him. The desperation of hearing me in the barn and not being able to get my attention. The torture he experienced at the hands of Carman during her possession of him. And perhaps most of all, the very recent death of Dad.

I grip the crystal hanging around my neck and focus on transferring my own sadness at the tragic loss of a father I only recently discovered I had into the crystal so that Scott's sadness won't cripple me when I try to ease it. He still doesn't know about Calliope's betrayal a decade and a half earlier, and I will never tell him. That is one secret I will take to either my grave or the Otherworld. I reach for him. I may only be a reincarnated version of the Goddess Brigit, with only a fraction of her actual power, but still my touch soothes others. If I could remove all his pain I would, but to comfort him for a little while is all I can do, and I will do it freely with as much love and compassion as I can muster. I knead his shoulders, working away the knots, but his mind will not be taken off course.

"Gigi, who is he?"

I sigh and sit down with my tea. If he doesn't want to be comforted, at least I can be. "You are stubborn and single-minded."

"Takes one to know one."

"What are we, twelve?"

He sits across from me. He is uniquely annoying, and by that I mean he's the only one who can drive me crazy, push all my buttons, and still not have his balls kicked in or his kneecaps taken out.

"You haven't answered my question."

There's still time for physical injury, but I decide to answer him. I owe him that much.

"His name's Alaric, and we've been hanging out the past few days."

"Define 'hanging out,'" he says. He even adds air quotes.

I roll my eyes.

"I'm waiting . . ."

I'm not going to get into the entire backstory about Alaric watching me for weeks in Vernal Falls or that he was my dance partner at Metropol the night I passed out for two days after, and the one who saved me after Breas almost killed me on the way to Radley Pond, because even in my head it sounds stalkerish.

"We met at a club last week. He brought me home safe and sound. We've been close ever since."

He scowls at me. He knows all too well what I've done with strangers I've just met in the past. "Define 'close.'"

"Scott!"

"Define 'close,'" he says again.

I pull my lips in. I missed him more than anything, but I forgot how much of a pain in the ass he can be too.

You know I will find out one way or the other.

"We didn't have sex."

We certainly tried, but we kept getting interrupted. Stupid universe, interfering with our plans.

The not-having-sex part seemed to appease him, at least during dinner and the remainder of the evening. Granted he had a lot of other things on his mind. I tried not to read him. I really did. But being separated from him for so long and almost losing him made it impossible for me to stay out of his head. I kept getting sucked back in whenever I tried to withdraw from it. His mind always returned to the deaths of Dad and Calliope and Ryan, and how fucked up the entire situation was. He also wondered why I keep denying I'm the reincarnated goddess. He heard me confess that I was Brigit to Clayone, but later, when Scott asked me, I told him that I had lied—the seering throat was worth it to avoid acknowledgement of a truth I'd like to keep to myself.

Of course, he doesn't believe me. He also doesn't know what my motivation is for denying my true identity, especially with Clayone imprisoned. The fact is, my brother doesn't need to carry the burden of my truth. No one does. I will continue refusing to admit I am the reincarnated goddess. The more time that passes from my I-am-Brigit epiphany, the more likely my violent tendencies will return and I'll kick someone in the shin when they try to say I am the Goddess.

Granda left us after dinner to attend to some errands. And by errands, I assume he means getting rid of dead bodies. He didn't go into details and was very hush-hush about what they had been up to all day. I tried to focus on his mind, but I've never been able to read him. Either he's blocking me somehow or there are some people I just can't tune into. I wish I knew why I can read certain people but not others.

Scott adds another log to the fire. The flames dance and lick at it. Sparks jump out at him, and he swats them away with a small metal shovel. The distraction is good for both of us because, while he tries to avoid lighting the house on fire, my mind returns to Alaric. I can't stop thinking about him and what might have happened when he got home. Could he tell that Carman and Calliope were dead? Or that his father, Clayone, was gone forever too? Not dead, mind you, but locked in my shrine, and I am the only one with the power to release him.

The red-orange flames of the fire remind me of last night's Super Blue Blood Moon. Then my mind jumps to the next full moon and what might happen. Will Alaric turn into a werewolf? Is that the surprise Carman was alluding to? Is that who the nightlock is for? And probably the most pressing question, Will he want to kill me too?

Slipping Scott a sleeping potion was easy. He's always been entirely too trusting in my opinion. He drank all of the tea I offered him, then went to bed. As I waited for him to fall asleep, I fell back into our real-life horror movie scene. Him, lying there, dying. Me, slicing my palm, pouring my blood into the healing chalice. Me, making him drink my blood. His body convulsing before falling still. Me, thinking I'd killed him. Him, returning to life. Me, going to Dad, begging him to drink from the chalice. Dad refusing. Telling me, "No." That he wanted it that way.

Why did he refuse to drink? Why did he choose to leave me?

He mentioned something about it only working once a day, but how can that be? Why would magic come with a limitation? What good is a healing chalice if it can't heal everyone at any time?

And what happened to it?

It was in my hands, but when the cow licked my cheek, all the memories of my past lives of Brigit disappeared, along with the chalice.

If there really is a "storm" coming, I need that bowl. And unless those cows can talk, I need to speak with the one person who can help me. The Goddess herself.

I count slowly backward, allowing myself to slip into a semiconscious meditative state. When my breathing slows, I call to the voice in my head, the voice I now know is Brigit. She doesn't answer. I try again, over and over, but I get nada. Zilch. Zero. I slip deeper and deeper into a meditative zone, but still, Brigit won't answer me. The Goddess is as stubborn as the living, breathing Gigi Brennan—she'll give me answers only when she wants to.

Thanks for your help, I shout at her so loudly I yank myself out of the meditation.

You're welcome, she laughs.

I groan. It's just my luck that the voice in my head appears to ride the turbulent wave of sarcasm with me, and now my little trip down memory lane and my attempt to commune with my obstinate alter ego failed to produce one iota of meaningful information and lost me precious time with Alaric. Scott's got to be asleep by now.

I walk over to the window, but instead of immediately climbing out, I stare at the Celtic knot tapestry serving as a makeshift curtain. I draped it over the curtain rod when I first arrived in Ireland to darken the room. It's one of the only mementos I brought with me from Vernal Falls, but it's not home it reminds me of. It's Lizzie. In seventh grade when we were supposed to be touring the Carnegie Science Center along with the rest of our class, we snuck into a head shop. I fell in love with the intricate Celtic design. Yes, I've been woefully ignorant of my true identity for a very long time. I may be gifted at many things, but I'm best at the art of the denial.

Anyway, I had to have it, but it was twenty dollars and I only had fifteen. I thought about stealing it but wasn't quite sure how to go about doing it since the tapestry was hanging from the wall. Without me asking her, Lizzie handed me six dollars. I tried to give her a dollar back, but she said, "There's probably tax. Keep it."

That's the Lizzie I remember. Always practical and giving to her own detriment—she only had six dollars, and we were supposed to buy our own lunches. We went hungry that day, but the tapestry was worth it. I hung it right up on the wall when I got home, and the two of us would lie on the floor and stare at it for hours sometimes not even talking.

A lone tear trails down my cheek. I swipe it off. There's no point mourning the dead when there's still living to do. I push aside the tapestry and climb out the window. Of course, the front door would be easier, but where's the fun in that? And since I'm mostly Gigi, with a touch of goddess, risk-taking keeps me sharp. I need to retain as much of my points and barbs as possible. I do have a reputation to maintain.

Sneaking out to see Alaric seems like both a brilliant idea and the stupidest thing I've ever done, and I've spent sixteen years doing stupid things. I didn't even take the time to think about what his true nature could be. What it most likely is.

If Clayone is indeed his father, he must be a werewolf too. And not just any werewolf, the son of the Original Werewolf. The very one I laid the curse of the full moon and the silver bullet on. The very one I imprisoned for all eternity. Well, my immortal form did anyway. I guess I'm guilty by association.

And what about his mother? He mentioned she died in childbirth, which fits with one of the werewolf creation methods in that freaky manual Carman had me read my first night in Kildare.

I never had the chance to know my mother, and I only discovered Uncle Mark was my dad when it was too late. Maybe I was too hasty imprisoning Clayone. Maybe there was another way. Maybe the third curse—the nightlock, the herb that can prevent the change—could have prevented Clayone from killing me. Maybe I didn't need to lock him away from Alaric for all time . . .

Before I can begin regretting yet another decision I've made in my life, I shrug it off.

If I hadn't imprisoned Clayone, I'd be dead. And though I would have gladly given my life for my family, they didn't leave me a choice. Most of them departed this world long before I was ready for them to go. Before I could even say goodbye. Before I even knew who I was.

But now's not the time to dwell on the bad especially with Alaric waiting for me. Courage and hope surge within me. Everything with Alaric will work out. It has to.

My nostrils fill with the scent of rain on a hot summer day just as an Irish voice I swore I'd never hear again yells out into the darkness. "Running away or running to?"

I swerve away, hoping to avoid Breas without incident, but it's as if he's read my mind. He steps out of the inky black night and grabs me.

3

ALMOST MIDNIGHT KISSES

*T*he moonlight streamed into the greenhouse, marking her arrival. She came to me as I knew she would. She, like all females, cannot resist my charms. In this reincarnated form, she is pliable, and I will bend her to my will.

We are all granted gifts. It is how we use them that matters.

"You betrayed me last night."

"I didn't." She lifts her chin. Even in her sleeping form, she dares to defy me. She's far stronger than I've given her credit for.

"You breathe fire."

"No, I didn't."

I reach for her. With my touch, she shall not hide the truth. "Who was it?"

She shakes her head, trying to rid herself of the foreign energy coursing through her. She knows not how to wield her power or withstand my own. "I don't know."

Her refusal stokes my anger. "Who. Was. It?"

"I don't know who it was, but I dream of him. He is what I desire. He is who I long for. Who I've always longed for."

She's lived many lives through the years, most of which she will

not remember, but if she's found the one she considers her true
mate, I will kill him. I've done it before. I will do it again.

"You forget yourself. It is I you long for."

She backs away from me. "No, I don't."

How is it that she brought her anger and hatred into this
reincarnation? Her feelings for me were to die with her celestial
form.

I close the distance between us and force my energy to fill her.
To compel her. "It is I you desire."

"It is you I desire," she says.

And I take possession of her lips that are rightfully mine.

WTF was that? Did I just slip into Breas's freaking mind? I
didn't even know I could do that. Maybe some residual
powers of the Goddess remain even if the memories are
gone. Or maybe since I can read minds, I can read memories
too. And if that's the case, that son of a bitch called me to the
greenhouse the night after I was at Metropol. The night
after I encountered Alaric for the first time. Breas compelled
me to forget Alaric and to adore him. He forced me to kiss
him. But he has no control over me now. The weak Gigi
who was passed around from one Dead Bastard bandmate to
the next last year is gone, replaced by a beautifully fierce
female, who will not be forced to do anything she doesn't
want to do.

"Take your filthy hands off of me."

He edges closer. "Is that any way to greet a lover?"

"You're no lover of mine," I hiss.

"Not in this lifetime. Not yet. But it's only a matter of
time, dear Brigit. The one I call 'Wife.'"

No freaking way.

Bile fills my stomach.

"Get your fucking hands off me."

He leans in so close his lips almost touch mine. "Or what? What will you do?"

I reach within myself for strength. Physical not magical. But I can't break his hold. His meaty hands are crushing my arms into my sides, bruising my muscles but not my spirit. He can never touch my spirit. In his relentless pursuit to restrain my upper body, he left my knees unattended. He forgot the damage I can cause with them. I jerk my left knee up between his legs to hit everything he thinks makes him a man. Before I can feel the satisfying crunch of smashed testicles, though, a rush of heat blasts past me and he's jerked away.

Alaric pins him to the ground. Breas tries to knock him off, thrashing his arms and legs. He bares his teeth. He hisses. Yells. Shouts. But Alaric won't release him. Won't let him move an inch.

The air crackles. Actually freaking crackles. Like what happens when magic's occurring, but I can't tell which one the conductor is. Neither one of their lips move to call the spell or curse.

"I'm going to kill you," Alaric growls at him.

"Not before I end you," Breas snarls through clenched teeth so white I have to look twice to make sure fangs aren't protruding from his canines. "You have no idea who you're dealing with."

"Funny," Alaric grunts, "I was just going to tell you the same. And considering I've got the upper hand, I'd say I'm winning."

Breas attempts to rise, but Alaric holds him firmly. It is a test of wills and strength, and I pray to the gods that Alaric wins. Breas tries again and again, failing every time. Finally, he falls back against the ground, panting. "Who are you?"

"Your worst nightmare."

Cliché, I admit, but given the circumstances I won't judge.

Their battle fascinates me—I know that's twisted and definitely sick. I'm supposed to be some peace-loving goddess, but I've never had two boys fight over me. Sure, Scott and Ryan knocked around guys who got a little handsy, but none of them ever fought back. They knew I wasn't worth the effort or the black eye. But these two? A gladiator death match would be less intense.

Locked physically, the air crackles again. There's a subtle shift, and they begin to engage in some type of mental warfare. Energy pulses from them. Raised by Carman and Calliope, Alaric must know dark magic spells and incantations.

Breas's eyes widen in surprise. He murmurs what must be a counter spell. Alaric's grip loosens before he realizes what's going on and clamps back down.

So, Breas knows magic too. He suggested as much all those weeks ago when Lizzie, dear sweet Lizzie, stole the spell book and tried to curse Kensey. There's something powerful about his type of magic. Similar to Carman's Maleficium. But that also must be the type of magic Alaric is using.

The night sky rumbles and the heavens open up, releasing rain. Strong winds whip across the fields. I can't tell if it's natural or one of them called it.

A crack of lightning splits the darkness, hitting inches from their heads. Thunder follows, shaking the very earth on which they lie. Tremors rock the surface as if the ground will split open and swallow us into the fiery pits of hell, and I am paralyzed to stop it.

Scott flies past me. "What the hell's going on?" He yanks on Alaric's back. Alaric's body shudders and jerks as if spelled. Breas takes advantage of the weakness and knocks him off. The two leap up and charge each other, but Scott blocks them. "Enough!" he shouts. His warning carries weight, as if with the strength from the Otherworld itself. I know we're witnessing Oegden's power, and he is a mighty being to behold. The storm even parts for him, leaving a clear night sky where once rain fell.

They both back away, eyeing each other but wary of him.

"What is the meaning of this?" he demands.

Alaric and Breas pace around him, neither one answering.

"Gi? What happened?" he says.

At the mention of my name, Alaric and Breas stop circling. They don't break their death stare to look at me, but I sense their emotions—or at least their testosterone—trying to claim me.

Anger washes over me. I may not be able to harm anyone with only my defensive spells, but I can still be a real bitch. I refuse to be claimed as a piece of property.

They each take another step back, sensing my wrath.

Good. They better back the fuck up.

"Breas grabbed me, and before I could break away, Alaric knocked him to the ground."

Scott turns to Breas. "You grabbed my sister?"

Breas smiles. His stance loosens. "So, you know now?"

Scott, tell him nothing.

Like I'd tell anyone the truth. You won't even admit it to me.

"That Gigi's my sister? Yes, but it's none of your concern. I don't care if she's my sister or my next-door neighbor or just a random girl on the street. You will never touch her without her permission. Understand?"

"Oh, come on, Scott. You know her," he says.

Alaric lunges at him. Scott throws up his arm to block him. He stumbles backward, stunned. I knew my brother was strong but, sheesh.

"I'll get to you in a minute." The force of Scott's words softens Alaric's aggression. "Thank you, Alaric," he says politely. Only Scott would call upon his manners in times of epic struggles. He shifts his attention back to the source of all the trouble. "Breas, you listen to me. You keep your hands off my sister, or I will break them."

Breas's eyes narrow. As if saying, "I'd like to see you try," but he keeps his mouth shut. At least he can be taught—or temporarily tamed. He is nothing but trouble. I know it.

"Now, Alaric, how do you know Gigi?"

Scott wants to find out if I was telling the truth or not. He truly is the most stubborn pain in the ass I know.

For the first time since the battle began, Alaric's green eyes meet mine. The anger I felt toward him trying to claim me slips away, replaced by something else. Calmness I think. "We met a few days ago, but we've known each other a very long time."

We have known each other before. Another lifetime I think. A time before this one. But how do I explain that to him or Scott without acknowledging who I am?

Scott walks over to me and takes my hand. "I'm taking Gigi home. I don't give a shit what you two do to each other, but you're not doing it in front of my sister."

Breas tries to follow Scott. "I'll go with you."

Alaric steps up beside me. "I will too."

Scott throws up an energy blast or a shield. Yeah, it feels like a shield—blocking but not attacking. Alaric and Breas fall back. Ironically, I don't even think Scott realizes he did it. He's so angry and focused on getting me away from potential danger that he'll do whatever's necessary to keep me safe. "Neither one of you are coming. Go to your home or whatever hole you live in. Breas, I don't know what happened to you all those weeks ago, and we certainly need to talk about a number of things, but now's not the time or the place."

Breas opens his mouth as if to argue. Scott stiffens, and he closes it. "Fine. Tomorrow then?"

Scott nods.

Alaric lifts my hand. "Tomorrow then?"

I fall into the hypnotic feel of his lips caressing my hand. He entrances me.

Scott clears his throat, and the spell lifts. "Alaric, come to the house tomorrow. We're having a serious conversation before I let my sister anywhere near you."

I try to pull away from Scott. "You're not the boss of me."

He tightens his hold. "Yes, I am. Now, let's go."

As he leads me away, I glance over my shoulder. Breas and Alaric face off in a silent war of wills. "Scott, we can't leave them. They'll kill each other."

He keeps walking. "Not my problem."

I struggle to keep up with him. I don't remember him being so freakishly strong. "Scott, slow down. Can we talk about this?"

He pulls me along. "When we're safe inside the cottage, we can talk, but until then, silence."

"I don't find this side of you very flattering."

He glares at me. "Gi, I don't know who Alaric is, but he's trouble. He looks at you like you're his."

"You've got a lot of nerve passing judgment on someone you don't even know."

I mean, sure Alaric's dad is Clayone, and he was raised by Carman and Calliope, but that doesn't make him a bad person. He's done nothing but be nice and caring to me, and that should count more than all the other crap put together. Besides, Scott doesn't need to know his entire backstory. His actions speak volumes.

"He protected me from Breas."

And it wasn't the first time.

Scott keeps pulling me along, but I can tell I've peeked his interest. But how do I tell him that Alaric's been my guardian angel since Vernal Falls? To admit that he was my mysterious dance partner at the club. The reason why I got home after Breas abandoned me at Radley Pond. And all the other times when he was there and no one else was. Or even to explain this notion, this flash of memory, of another time and place, of another life of Brigit, even though all the memories of my past lives disappeared with the lick of the cow.

"If he shows up tomorrow, I might give him a chance, but there will be rules and provisions, and he will need to be extremely convincing."

I look back one more time. The night sky ate everything in its path including the silhouettes of Alaric and Breas. As much as I don't like Scott telling me what to do, it was a relief he showed up. Watching Alaric and Breas fight over me was shit-ass scary. I mean, sure I was oddly fascinated by it in the beginning, but if Breas had gotten the upper hand, he'd think he won me, and he will never win me.

And if Alaric won and Breas lay in a crumbled heap, the two of us would be alone together. The kissing would be hot and delicious. But what if he wanted to talk about his dead nan or aunt. Or his missing dad? I'd have to lie to him. Act sympathetic and surprised that all of the people in his life disappeared. And even though they were insane Maleficium sorcerers, I know how it feels to lose the ones you love. That feeling bites hairy ass.

"Scott?"

He opens the door to the cottage for me. "Yes?"

I pull on my crystal to give me courage to admit I was wrong to him. "I'm sorry I slipped you sleeping potion."

He glares at me. "I thought the tea tasted different."

I pull my lips to the side in my mischievous grin. "Can't blame a girl for wanting to hang out with her boyfriend without her brother stalking her. But I am curious how you woke up. You should have been knocked out until at least midmorning."

His eyes widen. "Midmorning? Don't you feel the least bit guilty about knocking me out?"

I smile. "Not really."

He sighs. He can't stand that I'll never be shamed into admitting any wrongdoing. "Fine. If you must know, I suddenly woke up from a deep sleep and knew you were in trouble."

"How did you know where to find me?"

He shrugs. "I just started running, without even thinking about where I was going, and heard a ruckus. I knew you couldn't be far off."

I stare at him for a long time, so long it should get uncomfortable for us both, but it doesn't. Not in the least. "Thanks."

"That's what I'm here for, Gigi. That's what I'll always be here for."

4

LOVERS' EMBRACE

*S*he hid the truth from me. She acted as if she possessed neither the Grimoire nor the power to access the spells and curses. She lied to me, just as she lied about her Friday night liaison.

How is it that she remembers her lust and hatred for me, but remembers not who she is? What have they told her about her heritage? What lies have they spun?

And who or what found her Friday night? I've not felt the presence of another since I arrived here, but her lack of memory and her refusal to acknowledge the identity of her partner suggests powerful dark magic—I know only one who possesses such power.

And I will have her head if she plots against me.

Kensey finds me at the bottom of the stairs of the school where we arranged our meeting. This building is a dark and dreadful place, so different from the paradise I left behind.

"Breas, love, what's wrong?" She slides her hands onto my shoulders and kneads the muscles.

"It's nothing."

"You're so tense. Let me help you forgot your worries."

"Where did Gigi say she was going?"

She stiffens, though she knows better than to show anger at me or my question. It is not something I've taught her. She reacts on intuition. She knows my desires and my wants as I know hers. We pair well together.

She fingers her lips. "She said nothing."

"Did you like it when she kissed you?"

She returns her hands to my shoulders. "I like when you kiss me."

The evasion of the question means little to me. It matters not. She will be a part of my harem, and Gigi will be the leader.

"Shall we go for a ride on my bike?"

She smiles, taking my hand. "What are we waiting for?"

This afternoon I will indulge with Kensey.

Tonight I will remind Gigi how powerful human emotions are.

Nightmares have long haunted my sleep, but I have never slipped into the mind of another. Now, after my encounter with Breas and his touch, it's like I become him or at least shift into his mind for a short time. And that mind is a twisted, psychotic place to be. How does he know who I am? He knew about magic and the spell book. Did he take Kensey and the "Grimoire," as he called it? And who interfered with his plans?

And who is he to me? Gram and Dad indicated a connection. A connection I've avoided, ignored, been repulsed by—take your pick. But the nagging sensation that I've been close to him yet also hate him remains.

So many freaking questions and so few answers. I should just spend my days and nights in bed. I'd avoid a lot of drama that way. Maybe the "storm" will pass overhead and blow out to sea, and I'd be none the wiser. Sounds like a brilliant plan to me. Avoidance. I like it.

I stretch in bed before making myself comfortable under

the blankets. I wonder how long I could get away with avoiding the world before Scott drags me out by the ear and makes me interact with people. Granda would probably let me go for a few days. Clarissa might allow a day or two. But Scott? That big oaf will drag me out kicking and screaming.

Rather than make a scene first thing in the morning, since I made a wonderful one in the middle of the night, I crawl my lazy ass out of bed and wander into the kitchen. On the counter there's a cup of tea waiting for me. This gesture makes me both happy and sad. Happy that I still have people in my life who care for me. Sad that Gram, the one who cared for me the most, is no longer with me. For so many years I felt alone, and I shouldn't have. Truth is, I've never been alone. But it wasn't until I confronted Scott's death that I realized that. That I realized how lucky I am.

Oh my god—I've turned from a freaky unemotional orphan into a sappy disaster zone. Grab your life preservers and rafts because the floodgates could open at any time.

Leave it to self-absorbed me to take so freaking long to figure out I've always been surrounded by love and loyalty. Even Lizzie, my best friend, stood up for me whenever some dillweed started talking smack about me behind my back— and I'm sure that happened on a daily basis. Lizzie. My dear sweet Lizzie. I miss her most of all. Gram, at least, was old and lived a long, full life. Dad, at least I could say goodbye to. But with Lizzie . . . I don't know . . . I feel like her story isn't over yet. Like it isn't finished. The day of her funeral she told me she was summoned. Summoned by who? Not the Goddess Brigit, that's for sure, because if it was, she'd be here by now.

In my soul I know I am Brigit reincarnated, but in my mind I'm Gigi Brennan, disturbed sixteen-year-old girl who lies, cheats, and steals. A girl who lost her mother, her father, her grandmother, and two of her best friends. A girl who has made innumerable mistakes and will make a shit-ton more before she's through with this existence.

I bring the tea to my lips, ready to continue drifting through my memories a while longer but, alas, as seems to be my life these days, there's always someone waiting for me who wants to talk about *something*.

"Oh, good," Granda says. "I'm glad you're up. We must discuss your plans."

I nearly spit the tea out. "Plans? What plans?"

Scott walks out of Dad's room. "Our plans for school."

I bring the tea back to my lips. No point on it going cold for crap like this. "School? Are you serious? Do you think I care about school? I'm not going back to Vernal Falls. There's nothing for me there."

"I agree," Granda says, "but it is an option. We can spend the school year in Vernal Falls and the summers here."

I shake my head. "No, I don't think so."

Granda pulls up a chair. "Gigi, you're not the only one in the family. Decisions are made democratically and sometimes with compromise. Scott, what would you like to do?"

Scott sips from his own mug. I know now that Gram's tea suppresses my magical abilities. It must suppress his too, but I don't think I'll tell him. Let him live a nonmagical life for a while longer. God knows I'm trying to repress all magical elements as long as I can.

"I don't think Gi's capable of compromise. Fortunately, she can't shoot fireballs out of her eyes either."

And there he is.

"Well, at least I don't shoot gas balls out of my ass."

"Next time we eat bean casserole let's see who worries about matches lit near their butts."

"Children!" Granda says. We immediately quiet down. "Is

this the type of conversation I can expect from you while you live with me?"

Scott winks at me. "Yes. We like to keep things light."

"Or gaseous."

Granda smacks his head with his hand. "What did I get myself into?"

"A lifetime of wonderment and comic relief," Scott offers.

Granda chuckles to himself. "My dear Rose is laughing at me. She in no way prepared me for this part of your journey."

It's the first time he's mentioned Gram in actual conversation other than when I guessed he was my grandfather. There's so much I want to know about Gram. For instance, what was she like when she was younger, and why did they decide to stay apart? Why did Gram lie to me about my grandfather? How many more secrets were left unsaid, lying in wait, preparing to rip my throat out?

"Children, can we get back to the conversation at hand?"

Scott scratches his head. "Sure . . . what were we talking about again?"

"School?"

Scott nods. "Right. I don't know what I want to do. Football season's over, and without Ryan there, I don't know if I would even want to go back. With Dad and Gram gone, what's left for us in Vernal Falls?"

His eyes start to water. Mine burn. A sympathy reflex true, but his losses are my own too.

"I . . . ," I begin, but my train of thought is interrupted by someone knocking at the door. Scott narrows his gaze at me.

"What?"

"I wonder who that can be?" he says, sounding annoyed and slightly threatening.

I stick out my chin. "We don't know who it is."

He glares at me.

"Who is it?" Granda asks as he walks over to the door and opens it.

There, standing before him, is Alaric.

Granda offers him his hand. "Good morning, Alaric. I'm Amorin. It's nice to finally meet you after hearing so much about you," he says, winking at me with that impish twinkle in his eye.

We didn't speak about him so much as he "witnessed" Alaric in my mind during our Otherworld journey in the gardens.

"He knows about him?" Scott whispers.

I lift my mug. "More or less. Now, if you don't mind, I'd like to speak with Alaric *alone*, please."

He pushes up from the table. "Not without me, you don't."

"Pushy. Pushy. Come on. Granda is fine with him. Maybe you should be too."

He rolls his eyes and pushes past me. "I'll be the judge of that. Alaric, can we speak outside, please?"

"Scott, don't."

Granda looks back and forth. He doesn't possess the ability to read minds, but he's an expert at assessing body language.

"Gi, will you wait here while Alaric and I discuss some things?"

Alaric raises an eyebrow in question. As much as I love arguing with Scott, he is especially tenacious about anything that revolves around my welfare. After last night I don't know if he'll ever let me out of his sight. I beg a silent "please?" at Alaric, careful not to plant the word in his head— if I can even do that with him.

"See you in a few," he promises.

His wink melts me from the inside out.

· · ·

After an excruciating long time, Alaric manages to survive Scott's interrogation and is deemed worthy to interact with me on a temporary basis. Scott permits us to walk around the gardens outside the cottage but no farther. The rebel in me considers throwing obscenities at him, including rapid-fire intervals of my middle fingers in his face, but the other part, the sister part that is relieved at having him with me after being separated for weeks, at having him alive to order me around, at having him as my protector even when I don't want protection, leads me to keep my mouth shut, keep my fingers clamped into tight balls, and follow his instructions.

Together, Alaric and I wind our way through the herb gardens. "Your brother's intense."

"That's one word for it."

I kneel down to adjust the bell jar over the nightlock seeds I sowed the other day. I planted them as a preventive measure in anticipation of potential werewolf encounters sometime in the future. Of course, I dreamed of a far-off future, perhaps centuries from now when we've turned to dust. Now it seems the nightlock might help keep Alaric from going wolfish at the next full moon, and maybe keep him from killing me, which I really would appreciate. Later today, I'll make a garden bed in the shape of the crescent moon to honor the nightlock and my dedication to preventing the change from taking place. But discussions of werewolf tendencies will not be held with Alaric this morning. Or any morning or night, if I can help it.

Denial, I welcome you.

"You never mentioned he was coming to Ireland. You said he was back in the States in juvie."

I don't want more lies to separate us, but I can't tell him the truth. At least not the majority of it. "He was released, and since Granda is his guardian, he flew over."

I wait for the burn in my throat, but it doesn't come. I told Alaric the truth—it just wasn't the whole story.

We pass through the garden gate and meander toward the pond. All right, so I can't follow Scott's directions exactly. At least we're still within view of the cottage where I'm sure he's watching our every move. As if to prove the point, his bedroom window curtains skirt to the side. His big hulking frame stands on the other side of the glass with his arms folded. It's his contemplative, ready-to-strike, Captain America pose.

Alaric, unaware of our chaperone, picks up a pebble and skips it across the water. Then he picks up a handful and fires them in quick succession.

I'm dying to ask him about Carman, Calliope, even Clayone . . . , but I need to be careful. He can't know the role I played in any of it. That was the deal Scott and I silently agreed on when he returned with Alaric after questioning him.

"So," I say, reaching for my own stones, "how was Halloween for you?"

That's it, Gigi. Act like you don't even know what a Sabbat is, let alone the name for it.

He skips a flat stone seven times before it finally swan-dives.

"Good one." I try to copy his technique, but I only manage three skips.

"It was all right. Not too painful. Better now that I'm here with you."

"Painful? What do you mean by that?"

He shifts away from me in search of more rocks. "Nothing."

I follow him along the bank. "Do fans get aggressive? Do they throw things?"

He laughs, but he sounds tired. Like there's no joy in him.

"No, nothing so dramatic. It's just a very long night. How was yours?"

It's my turn to move away. "Oh, you know. Nothing exciting."

A slow burn creeps up my throat.

"Tell me," he pleads, reaching for me. The instant our hands touch, a spark ignites. We stare at each other. An unspoken acknowledgment of all the things we're not ready to share with the other passes between us. For this moment, it doesn't matter what our truths are. We are bound together in a way neither one of us understands. I bury my head into his chest, allowing his heat to penetrate into my soul. His heart races with my proximity.

I don't know if he's a werewolf. I don't care if one day, maybe even today, he'll want to kill me. Alaric is real, and I've never felt so complete.

"I've needed this," he whispers, nestling me closer.

"Me too," I whisper back. "Me too."

5

WOLFIE CONFESSIONS

*W*e stand for a long time, holding each other. Becoming stronger together than apart. The lies, the secrets . . . none of it matters as we soak each other in.

"I can't believe your brother allowed us to hug for so long," he whispers to me.

I break away from him. "You saw him?"

"Hard to miss him standing in front of the window staring at us. His beady eyes burned two holes through my back."

"He's a little overprotective of me."

"I appreciate him watching over my siofra."

"So, I'm back to being your siofra again, even after last night."

"You will always be."

Most of my dating knowledge derives from books and Hollywood, but I'm pretty sure Alaric just made a lifetime commitment to me. That both thrills and frightens me. I mean, I feel the same way, sure, but I'm sixteen. He's eighteen. I may be a goddess, but I'm not ready for an official vow to him. It all seems very Romeo and Juliet-esque, and even though he promised me we're not in an English tragedy, I can't help but wonder if maybe we're in an Irish one.

Instead of verbally confirming his pledge to me or adding my vow to his, I pull my lips to the side and wink.

He laughs. "I'll get you yet. Now, let's sit and catch up, because according to your brother, I'm 'skating on thin ice,' and when I disputed him by saying that it was only November and the ice won't form until at least December, he didn't find my joking particularly charming."

The Scott I've grown up with and the Scott other people meet are often two very different beings. "He's typically the master of bullshit. Give him time."

He brushes a lock of hair behind my ear. "I intend to. Now, the real reason I'm here, other than wanting to spend every possible waking moment with you, is to invite you over to my house for a proper dinner tonight."

I swallow hard, preparing my throat for the inevitable scalding it's about to receive. "To your place?"

He nods.

Play it cool, Gigi. Play it cool. "Will anyone be joining us?"

He winks at me. "Not a one. My auntie's away, and my nan disappeared, but she's done that before. She does these . . . ," he pauses and shifts his gaze to me. "You know she's a witch, right?"

Was a witch.

I nod.

"She goes on spiritual journeys to the Otherworld."

I nod again to confirm I know exactly what he's talking about.

"Sometimes she actually visits the Otherworld physically. Before I left, she told me she might not be here when I got back—that's why she wanted me to stay, but it wasn't safe to."

I lean toward him. Ready for him to reveal a secret tied to

the full moon. He knocks his shoulder into me instead. "And my dad was a no-show anyway. Big surprise."

Not surprising at all, actually.

"So much for looking forward to seeing his son." Under the bitterness lies a sadness that makes me hurt for him. Makes me regret inadvertently hurting him.

"Why did he want to see you?"

Alaric skips another rock. "I'm his son."

I study the gentle ripples left in the wake of it and try to let our conversation die, but just like the tiny ripples of the rock, I can't stop the momentum. "Yes, but why after all these years?"

He pulls away from me. "I thought you of all people would understand."

I understand that a father-son meeting will never take place, but I can't tell him that. He pushes his hands through his hair as he sighs in frustration. My silence isn't helping him calm down.

"Nan mentioned something about my dad wanting forgiveness. What if he shows up and I can't forgive him? The parts of me I hate the most are because of him. You're the only light in my life."

We're on the precipice of confession, and though I knew it would someday come, I'm not ready for it.

"I'm not the only light in it."

His green eyes spear my heart. "You are. There are things I've done that I'm not proud of. Things I don't remember, and I want to. I want to be good for you, but something pulls me—I can't describe it. It's like I lose my mind."

A weight falls on my shoulders, and I wrap it around me as if I can ward off the truth of what he's about to tell me.

"Sometimes I wake up in the morning, and I can't remember where I've been. I can't remember what I've done. There's mud on my shoes and blood on my hands."

"Blood?" I whisper. "What kind of blood?"

"I don't know."

"How do you not remember?"

"I don't know. I want to be good. I really do, but sometimes I have this feeling that I've done horrible things. Terrible things."

"What kind of things?" I whisper.

"I don't know, Gi. I don't know."

He wraps me into another hug. The conflict swirling around inside of me is a mighty, wretched thing.

He left soon after his almost confession. Not by choice but by necessity. Scott threatened to tear off his limbs if he didn't leave immediately. I have to be honest. My brother's threat of violence surprised me. Scott's generally much more cordial, but something changed him on Samhain. It changed us both.

As I watched Alaric lope off into the distance, he reminded me of a wolf. Not the intimidating werewolf of his father, but a gentle, loving wolf that only cares about protecting his pack. A wolf who would never harm another living soul if he could help it.

When his silhouette is nothing but a speck, Scott turns to me. "Gigi, spill every last detail. Every last stinking detail."

I wander back down the pond embankment and skip another rock at its edge. "Scott, please don't ask me. Can't you just trust me?"

He reaches for my hands. His green eyes spear me just like Alaric's, but in a different way. "Gi, you're the only family I have left."

Still I resist. "What about Granda?"

"You are my family. I need to know."

I release a sigh. Only Scott can wear me down and guilt me into telling him anything he wants to know. I sit on a stump and pat the one beside it. "Might as well make yourself comfortable. It's going to be a while."

"So, Alaric," he says.

"Right," I reply, but before I can even start, Breas shoves me over and sits beside me on the stump.

"Well, if it isn't my favorite people in all of Ireland."

I am in no mood to touch or be touched by Breas again. His creepy-ass visions will push me over the edge of the cliff I so precariously teeter along. I pull away from him. "I don't think so."

He reaches for me.

Scott blocks him. "Breas, you and I need to talk."

"Can Gigi stay and keep us company whilst I entertain you with Celtic tales of love and loss?"

"She will do no such thing. Gi," Scott says, glancing over at me, "would you mind going inside and waiting for me?"

He makes me laugh. He really does. Since his arrival in Ireland, his manners have reverted into a much more formal nature than when we were in Vernal Falls. And the best part is that he actually believes he can persuade me to listen to him, but the truth is I don't want to be anywhere near Breas.

"I'm more than happy to meet you, but I won't lock myself in my room. You know where to find me."

In the gardens.

He nods. "See you there."

Breas laughs. "When is it that you two will acknowledge that you can read each other's minds?"

"I don't know what you're talking about," Scott growls, "and I'm not here to talk about my relationship with my sister. I want to talk about you and how you're treating her."

Sensing that the conversation has shifted from politely threatening to if-you-don't-tell-me-what-I-want-to-hear-I-will-smash-your-face-in, I take my leave.

On my way back to Granda's cottage, I duck behind a tree

and watch them. Scott hasn't sat down yet, and from the looks of it, he won't anytime soon. By the erratic wave of his hands paired with the violent shaking of his head, he's telling Breas off for mistreating me. He doesn't know the half of it, but he's wasting his time. The tilt of Breas's head tells me that none of Scott's accusations have any effect on him whatsoever. He always has been and always will be a cocky bastard.

I close my eyes and try to focus on his brain—just to see if I can do it. Then I remember the way it felt to slip into his mind and witness his view of me and every other member of the female sex. Those visions I had of him weren't made up. They were real. They actually happened. That's some crazy-ass shit going on.

The air shifts. A warm breeze smelling of lavender and lemon verbena pulls me away from their conversation and far away from Granda's property. I told Scott I'd meet him in the gardens. I just didn't specify which one.

As if by magnetic pull, I run to the hidden garden that conceals Brigit's sacred well. I'm not planning to visit the Otherworld via the portal, but the answers to all my questions are waiting for me there. I know it. As I approach the trailing ivy "walls" of the garden, blood rushes through my veins in anticipation of spending time by myself in such a beautiful and meaningful setting. When I slip between the vines and enter the clearing, a calmness washes over me. The privacy of the gardens will allow me to meditate without interruption.

Or at least I'd hoped it would, but it appears someone else had the same idea.

Across from me on the far side of the clearing Alaric sits cross-legged with his head bowed before the pool of water. The very water I climbed out of when I returned from the Otherworld. Positive energy swirls around him. All light. All good. All Alaric. The water below him shimmers as an image forms.

Deep in his meditation, he's unaware that anyone's entered the garden. I don't want to interrupt him since I've learned to appreciate the importance of visions—but I'd like to see who or what he's "called." One, because this is Brigit's secret garden, and her portal, and since I've tried to "call" her a few times, and she's refused to accept my "calls," I figured she was currently out of service—especially since I'm the reincarnated version. And two, I'm nosey. I want to see what he's talking to her about.

I imagine myself invisible—I don't know if it actually works but in my mind it does—and then I chant in my head, "light as a feather," as I tiptoe around the pool in my impression of the ultimate creepiest stalker. When I get close, I peek over his shoulder.

A reflection of a beautiful gray and white wolf stares up at me from the still water with intense green human eyes. It's truth I see there. But not an ugly twisted truth. A pure one.

"You," Alaric whispers. "I knew it was you."

But he's not talking to me.

He's talking to my reflection standing behind the wolf.

6

SNEAK-OUT SNAFU

irt makes me happy. It clears my head. It soothes my soul. It gives me inspiration. Because of that, I returned to Granda's and got to work on the crescent moon garden. After the confusing scene with Alaric when he was talking to me, the goddess, but not actually to *me*, the person, I needed to get out of there as soon as possible. Sneaking away without him being aware of my presence was easy. Years of prowling around at night have served me well. I wouldn't say I'm proud of myself for spying on him, but then, I've spent a lifetime doing things I'm not proud of. Still, he was weak in his meditative state, and I took advantage of that.

Guilt rumbles through me, but not enough to make me go back and tell him what I witnessed. I'm not ready for him to see me for who and what I am.

But there's another thing I need time to mull over. I didn't feel scared in the wolf's presence. Well, his reflection. I felt like . . . like I belonged. Like we belonged. I don't understand how or why I felt that way. For a thousand years, his father has tried to kill me, to murder me, but he and I—

we've been together before. This I know with absolute certainty.

I pick up a smooth round rock and palm it back and forth as I walk back into Granda's garden. When I lay this final piece, my crescent moon garden bed will be sealed, and the nightlock will begin to grow.

After shifting the rock into position, I drop to my knees. The earth draws me back to the present. I pick up the trowel and start digging while trying to make sense of Alaric's existence. His dad is Clayone—that I know—but did Carman conjure him from the Otherworld as a reincarnated spirit to inhabit a werewolf body? She practiced Maleficium, but was she capable of such powerful magic?

Or did she create him? That book she gave me described in detail the different types of werewolves along with their origin stories and detailed explanations about which ones were the most obedient. I never questioned why she gave me the book. At the time I had no idea she meant me harm. I believed her words as deeply as Scott believes me about everything—even when I'm blatantly lying to him. But why did she give me the werewolf book? What did she want me to know? Is Alaric the surprise she warned me about? And is he still obedient to Carman or will he be loyal to me?

He will always be loyal to you.

Fan-freaking-tastic. The Goddess decides to reappear when it's convenient for her, and not when I ask her to.

In daylight he is yours.

In the deepest night he belongs to another.

Divided, he will break.

United, he will destroy that which tried to break him.

And now I'm spouting riddles like the Riddler. I mean, seriously. Like I don't have enough crap going on.

Go seek the one most dedicated to us.

She will guide you to the truth.

For in truth will come answers.

She means Clarissa. Clarissa knows far more than she shares with me or anyone else. I hope she'll tell me the truth rather than roundabout prophecies and snake-in-the-grass metaphors. I've had enough of that shit.

"Hey, stranger," Scott says, kneeling beside me. "I've been looking all over for you."

"I told you to meet me in the gardens."

"I checked all over the gardens, then I went to the Cathedral thinking that maybe you lied to me."

I pull my soil-covered hand to my chest. "Moi? I can't believe you'd accuse me of such treachery."

The soil grounded me back to the earth and my sarcasm. Let the world rejoice.

He rolls his eyes. "Where did you go?"

"I've been in the gardens the whole time." And only a slight burn to my throat—I suppose because I was vague in the exact location of the different gardens I'd been to.

"Uh-huh."

"How did it go with Breas? Did he reveal his evil deeds to you?"

His calm mind regarding Breas suggests he did not. "You really don't like him, do you."

"That's a gross understatement. I loathe him."

Scott knows me well enough to know that while I don't like most people, there are few I rank in the hate hate hate category. "Why?"

"Scott, he was hooking up with Kensey while he was hooking up with me. He physically harassed me a number of times, and he almost killed me on his motorcycle and left me for dead."

Scott leaps up. "What? When?"

Oh yeah, I neglected to tell him about that one, and evidently so did Breas. Big freaking surprise there. "It's ancient history now. I just don't like the guy and prefer to never see him again."

"I wish I knew that before . . ."

Oh no. I already know what he's about to tell me next, but I ask anyway because it makes me feel more sane. "Before what?"

"Before I invited him to dinner."

I jump up. "You did what?"

"Invited him to dinner."

It's times like these that I wish I could shoot fireballs out of my hands. The best I can do without resorting to violence —though the thought did cross my mind—is to roll my eyes in a dramatic way with my hands planted firmly on my hips. "It doesn't mean I need to be there. I have plans."

He enters my personal space, standing toe to toe with me. He is the only one willing to risk his life to make a point. He might know I can't physically hurt him with magic, but he knows my knees are capable of serious damage. "With whom?"

I wink at him in an effort to diffuse his anger but also to stoke it, because I thrive on contradiction. "Who do you think? Very private, very intimate."

He drags me into the back door of the cottage. "Nope, you're not going."

I struggle to break away from him. I mean, really. A goddess shouldn't be treated with such disregard. "You're not the boss of me, Scott. I'm going."

"Nope. Not going to happen," he says and pushes me into my room, slamming the door behind me. Before I can swing open the door and escape, he shoves a large object in front of it.

I lean into the door, but the darn thing won't budge. "Are you seriously locking me in my room?"

"Yes, I am."

"That's a fire hazard," I shout before I decide on a different tactic. Face to face I might be able to persuade him. I'd like to practice my compelling because I think it might be a residual Brigit skill I want to develop. I haven't had many opportunities to test the theory. "Can we at least talk about this?"

"Nope. You're not talking me into anything."

Come on, Scott. Don't be a doof.

"Nope, not doing it."

"Then I'm not coming to dinner."

"Well, I'm not bringing you food."

He enjoys cruel and unusual punishment entirely too much. "Granda won't let me starve. He'll let me leave." A weak attempt at guilt, but still, I had to try.

"Not if I tell him not to."

Evidently Scott thinks he might be able to compel people too. Unfortunately, he's not above using it to get what he wants, especially if it comes to ensuring my safety.

"You wouldn't dare."

"Don't dare me then."

An unfamiliar energy drifts over to me, distracting me from arguing with my brother. I glance around and realize someone's been in my room. Someone that wasn't invited. I look under my bed, check the closet, even pull out dresser drawers, but nothing seems to be out of place or missing. Not that I have anything worth taking, but I don't like people sneaking around my room. I close my eyes and try to read the energy signature. I'm new at the energy game, but who knows, maybe some goddessy voodoo remains and the remnant of the intruder will appear in the vapor. Mind you, most of my magical knowledge derives from TV series featuring witches and werewolves, but I figure some of those magical sequences have got to be based on research. I breathe in and out, allowing the energy to enter and float through my mind. It reminds me more of Alaric than anyone in my family, but it doesn't belong to him. Declan maybe? Did he sneak into my room in search of something that would turn Alaric against me? I keep breathing in and out with my eyes closed, trying to search for the source, but the afternoon sun isn't helping. It's entirely too bright in the room to concentrate on an energy signature.

And then I realize something.

My eyes flash open and stare at the open window. I overlooked the obvious. My tapestry's gone. Who in this world would take a tapestry? That's just ignorant.

I try to focus again on the energy, but now that I'm aware of what's missing, I also know that whoever snuck into my room is long gone and of no consequence to my present predicament. The open window, however, is begging me to sneak out of it in order to escape Scott's tyrannical rule. I quickly climb through with the full intention of disappearing before my know-it-all brother is any the wiser.

"Gotcha!" Scott leaps out in front of me.

I jump back, not expecting him in the least. I didn't even read his mind, which tells me I was completely distracted by uninvited guests and a missing tapestry. "Real original. Remind me not to volunteer you for a gig at a haunted house. You're the least intimidating person I know."

He raises his chin. "Intimidating enough to catch you."

I screw up my lips into a pout. "I can't believe you didn't trust me."

"Don't play the guilt game with me. I know how much you enjoy sneaking out."

"I'm shocked. I really don't . . . ," I shove him and run, hoping that surprise or divine intervention will rule in my favor and I can get to Alaric's for dinner.

Scott, however, is freakishly fast and catches me.

It's actually pathetic how fast he caught me. Speedy

getaways are not one of my strong suits, though dramatic attempted escapes definitely are.

I squirm around, trying to break his hold. "I didn't think you were good at catching things. I thought that's why you were the quarterback and Ryan was the runner guy who caught the balls you threw."

He rolls his eyes. "Really, Gigi, you'd think after all those games you sat through that you would have gained some basic sports knowledge."

"I'm uniquely immune to such trivia."

He shuffles me back into the cottage and guides me over to Dad's chair. Impressions of Dad sitting there reading calm me somewhat, but I'm really annoyed at Scott. I hate it when someone thinks they've outsmarted me.

"How do you expect to cook *and* keep me here? You're not going to tie me up, are you? There are laws against such cruelty."

"I'm fairly certain those laws don't apply to an obnoxious little sister who openly defies her older brother with little regard to the anguish and emotional exhaustion she put him through."

That sucked the wind right out of my airpipes. I slump back into the chair. "You're really going to play that card?"

He smiles at me. "I really am."

The front door opens. Granda steps to the side so Clarissa can walk in front of him. He takes one look at me clutching the arms of the chair as if I'm tied to it, then at Scott in the kitchen making a salad. "Did I miss something? Scott, did you magic your sister into the chair?"

Scott stops chopping the lettuce and looks up. "I can do that?"

Clarissa laughs as she sets a basket covered with a tea towel on the table. "The two of you are woefully undertrained and entirely too powerful. Tomorrow we begin magic school."

I wiggle my fingers at Scott. "I've always wondered if I could turn him into a frog, or wait . . . a swan—wasn't it a swan you turned into in order to find your true love?"

"Frog. Swan. Raven—a raven would actually be really cool. As long as I don't turn into a wolf. That hits a little close to home."

I get up and peek under the tea towel and admire the rolls Clarissa brought. "I don't think all wolves are bad."

"I assure you, my dear Gigi, all wolves are bad," Breas says, strolling in through the open door. "The Big Bad Wolf isn't just a character from a children's fairy tale."

"We really need to starting locking the front door so strangers don't wander in uninvited."

He stands beside me but, unfortunately, just out of striking range. "Oh, but Gigi, I was invited. By your beloved brother, in fact."

I sidestep further away from him. "Apologies, but I've got other plans. I'll be going."

"Gi," Scott calls out to me. "I thought we agreed that you'd stay for dinner."

His guilt manipulation swirls around me. I slump back into my chair. Scott can get me to do just about anything, the big oaf. I stare at him in annoyance, but my comment is directed at Breas. "I disagree about all wolves being bad, and I'll prove you wrong."

"You can try, but you won't succeed." I can tell he's smiling, and it just makes me more annoyed. My hands curl into fists. I don't like when someone tells me what I can and can't do. Especially Breas. I hate Breas and all his know-it-all-ness.

He steps in front of me and glances down at my curled

fists. His features soften as he looks at me. "I apologize. I've antagonized you. I did not intend to do that."

Huh. I didn't expect that. I had no idea he was capable of apologies or such modesty. That's surprising.

"Amorin, Clarissa," he says, bowing to them.

"Breas," Granda says. "Good to see you."

Clarissa nods but offers no other form of greeting. I try to read her mind, but she's closed off to me.

She glances my way and winks. Did she feel me poking into her mind?

I did.

Can you teach me how to close off my mind like that?

Where's the fun in that?

I roll my eyes. I can't believe the number of conversations I've had lately that take place entirely in my head. If I wasn't in my current company, I'd be committed for sure.

"Clarissa, I've brought you wine and biscuits for dessert."

She lays out napkins along with silverware. "It's not my meal or my house. Amorin and Scott would be the appropriate recipients of such hospitality."

"And what of Gigi?" His gray eyes try to penetrate my mind, but he won't get a read on me. I may not know how to close my mind to other people yet, but I've got no problem doing it with Breas.

"It wasn't my idea to invite you over. I had other dinner plans."

Scott clears his throat.

Be nice. He's trying to be nice to you.

"But, I heard you were coming and couldn't imagine a place I'd rather be."

Ever hear of too much bull?

Watch him buy it.

"Well, my dear Gigi, that is wonderful to hear," he says. "Will you do me the honor of sitting next to me?"

What I'd really like to say is, "Like I have a choice," but instead I keep my mouth shut and nod at him. "I'd be delighted."

If he wants to play as if we're in Victorian England with proper manners and proper courtships, then so be it. I shall be the Queen of Bullshit.

7

SCHMOOZE FEST

*S*cott made quick work of transforming the daily grab-and-go table into a candlelit delight. He wanted to do something nice for Granda and Clarissa since they've been so good to us. He's always done kind gestures like that.

Me, on the other hand, I've always been the selfish bitch who thinks of it after he's already planned something. Then I never follow through on my ideas, mainly because it would seem like I don't have a unique thought of my own.

Generosity of spirit is just one of the glaring differences that set us apart. I should try to do better, but I know I'm not going to change anytime soon. That's just the reality of the situation, and you know what? I'm fine with that. Keep expectations low. That way no one will be disappointed. Life motto to live by.

Clarissa and Granda drink wine while Breas charms the lot of us with tales of his youth in Ireland. His stories bear so little resemblance to Scott's and my own childhood experiences in Vernal Falls that it seems like much more than a country separated us. No one appears to notice this glaring difference except me though. I know this because I've been trying to read their brains the entire meal, and not even Scott seems to mind. Maybe I'm being hypersensitive—surprising I know—but his childhood can't be of this world. Maybe he's an alien from outer space. Green blood. Spewing venom. That would explain a lot, actually. A quick slice with Scott's dagger across Breas's palm would tell me everything, but no, Scott would probably frown upon bloodshed at the dinner table. The bore.

Granda and Clarissa literally eat Breas up as if he's more delicious than the biscuits he brought for dessert. Thankfully, there's a basket full of them. They'll be my consolation prize for surviving this torturous situation.

Scott, at least, watches him cautiously as he drinks his own glass of the wine. He's not sure whether to trust Breas's high spirits and put weight in his apology to me or chop him into little pieces and put him in the blender for wronging me. Sometimes I really love the way his mind works.

My own feelings for Breas are complicated. He and I are like oil and vinegar. I hate him. I want him. And if someone shakes the bottle hard enough, everything blends together into a confusing, almost romantic notion that I can't believe I'm capable of feeling for any person, let alone him and Alaric.

But then again, it should come as no surprise. I always want what's bad for me, and since Alaric has all but pledged himself to me, the thrill of the chase might be over. But with Breas, my conflicting emotions regarding him fascinate me. And the more wine I drink, the better he looks, and the less he annoys me.

His gray eyes catch mine and hold them for several long seconds. The shade reminds me of the ocean on a stormy day. Not that I've been to the ocean often—or at all actually. Being more than ten hours from the Atlantic makes the spur-of-the-moment skip day to hit the beach impossible. It's more of a memory of the ocean. I think at one time I loved it.

Kildare isn't far from the sea. Perhaps a day at the beach with Breas would clear my mind and help me figure things out . . .

"Where are you staying?" Granda asks him, breaking our connection.

I blink as Breas winks at me, satisfied that he's caught my attention at least for now. I'm left wondering where the hell the idea of me spending the day at the beach with him came from. I must be delusional.

"I've got an old cottage along the coast. I like to keep close to water."

Clarissa glances over at me. "I'm sure you do, but it's a far drive just to visit us. What brings you this way?"

Breas's gaze falls back to me. "I believe you all know the answer to that question."

He offers me the basket. "Biscuit, dear Gigi?"

I grab a chocolate one because, you know, chocolate. I am unashamed to admit that the fastest way to my fastidious heart is through confectionary delights. Granda and Clarissa polished off the rest of the wine during the meal, so we eat the biscuits with tea. I go for Irish breakfast tea rather than Gram's blend. It's time to drop the shields of my protection and fully face who I am, for better or for worse. Most likely for worse.

As the evening winds down and all the biscuits are gone, Breas turns to me and says, "Would you do me the honor of going for a stroll with me?"

And because he's been so charming and brought me delicious desserts, and because I am an idiot who gets herself into situations that are often slippery and treacherous, I agree to.

Scott yells in my head, *Are you sure? Are you sure you're okay being alone with Breas?*

I reply, "Yes."

"I'll be close by if you need me," he says aloud.

"May I?" Breas asks, gesturing to my hand.

I glance at it, then him, trying to figure out if this is an act or if he's truly sincere and trying to begin anew. I shrug. It's the most noncommittal answer I can give him. It puts all the control of his next actions on him.

He reaches for it, and I don't fight him.

This time when we touch, I don't slip into his mind. I don't want to kill him or argue with him. I'm actually drawn to him as if he serves as the missing piece of an intriguing puzzle. I wonder briefly if I've been spelled, but then, I don't really care because he's all shiny and different.

He leads me outside where the waning gibbous moon serves to remind us of its constancy.

"Gigi, please allow me to apologize for my behavior when we first met."

"Why are you talking like you're from another century? What happened to the cheesy one-liners, the rude comments, and the insinuating sarcasm?"

He smiles at me, his white teeth lighting up the night. "You miss them?"

"Well, maybe not the cutting remarks you made about me and Lizzie, but I've never had a problem with smart humor."

His forehead scrunches in an adorable I-don't-know-what-you-mean way.

"Sarcasm. Dry wit. Smart humor. All the same."

"Oh, well, then I will oblige you with it when I see fit. But, really, I do want to apologize to you for my behavior. I wasn't myself."

He doesn't need to explain his moodiness to me of all people. I survive on mood swings. Still, I won't make it easy for him. That would just be wrong. "And who were you then?"

He grins. "Would you believe I was from a foreign land?"

I pull him through the gardens. "Duh. You're from Ireland. Of course you were from a foreign land."

He guides me to the iron arch, leading us from the gardens to the pond. "Right. In denial still."

I'm not sure where he's going with this, but I need to curb him. "Not in denial. Just familiar with reality."

"You keep telling yourself that. Eventually you'll figure it out."

I know I should be annoyed with him for acting like he's the great Oracle of Knowledge, but when he turns to me, his gray eyes burn into mine, removing any desire to argue with him. In fact, I think I'd agree to whatever he asked of me.

"You look beautiful in the moonlight."

"Surprise, surprise. You're actually capable of a compliment. The last time you mentioned my appearance you wondered why I didn't bleach the black part of my hair to match the white."

"I didn't want to fill your head with flattery."

"I thought you were too busy with Kensey to worry about my ego."

He winks at me. "Ah, you were jealous."

I laugh, shifting away from him as we approach the bank of the pond. "I was no such thing. You were and are allowed to hook up with anyone you'd like. If brainless bimbos are your thing, then go for it."

"Kensey wasn't so much brainless as pliable. A trait I find admirable at times."

"Then you better keep a distance from me, because I am neither."

He laughs, but it's not a warm, hearty one that comes from the belly likes Scott's or Ryan's. It's a superficial, throat-deep one, and it doesn't draw me in at all. "Oh, I know that, Gigi. I am well familiar with your wily ways."

He talks as if we've had a long relationship, but we've barely interacted. "You don't know me that well."

"I beg to differ. But let's not argue over such trivial things. All I know is that I'd very much like to kiss you."

"You're actually asking?"

He steps over to me and reaches for my hands. "I am."

His gray eyes sparkle in the moonlight, and suddenly I want to kiss him too.

As his lips reach for mine, I hesitate and think about pulling away, but somehow he bends me to his will.

I don't resist him, which should set off the warning bells in my head, but for some reason it doesn't. Instead I kiss him, not feeling anything. Not passion. Not want. Not need.

Together we slip into another time, another place. I see us standing before an altar with a ribbon tied around our wrists joining us together, but I don't know why I chose this. I don't love him. I don't much care for him. Why would I bind myself forever? What purpose does it serve?

For peace. To settle the long, violent strife of your people.

But that was long ago. Much has been won and lost since.

I continue kissing him as if I don't hold possession over my own emotions, until I do. Anger and confusion wash over me. These feelings are also not my own, but they soon become mine. The weird radio frequency fuzziness fills my mind the same way it did when I thought someone was stalking me at school back in Vernal Falls. Well, actually when Alaric was stalking me, but I haven't felt that way since I arrived in Ireland. Could it be something I ate? Is that why I'm not resisting Breas?

A rock tumbles down the embankment, knocking into my foot. I break away from Breas. I kissed him far longer than I intended or even wanted to.

But yet, the image of us bound together was real. As real as the two of us standing together now.

My breath whooshes out of me as I realize we once shared a life together, or at least part of one. "Who are you to me?"

"You know who I am."

His gray eyes compel me to search within myself for the truth. I shut my mind to him, resisting whatever spell he tries to lay on me or whatever memory he wants me to remember.

"Gigi, it's time to come in," Scott yells from the cottage, further breaking Breas's connection to me. I immediately feel more like myself.

Breas leads me back up the bank before reaching to kiss my hand. "I shall bid you good night, dear Gigi."

The anger and confusion return. Betrayal stabs me at the base of my neck. I glance around, feeling like someone's watching us, but I don't see anyone in the darkness.

"Is everything all right?" he asks, his eyes peering into the night, searching for whatever might be lurking in the shadows.

I shift away from him. The air clears between us. "Yes, I'm fine."

And suddenly I am, or at least I think I am.

"Gigi, it's time!" Scott shouts from the house. His voice pushes me back to the present. "Say goodbye and get yourself inside."

His timing couldn't be more perfect, because I am a hotbed of disaster.

"I guess I'll be off. Unless, of course, you'd like me to stay." He tilts his body into me, and I drift back into him.

"Let's go!"

Fear of Scott's disappointment tears me away from Breas. "I better go deal with Scott and his accusations."

He pulls me in close. Enchantment settles back on my

shoulders. "If he accuses you of kissing me, he would be correct."

And that is a truth I won't lie about, because I'm sure Scott is watching us from a distance. "Yes, he would be. Good night, Breas."

"Good night, dear Gigi, and may your dreams be filled with beautiful magic," he says with a flourish of his hands. A weird magic-y kind of feeling falls over me, and I know that I've let the make-believe and reality combine together into a mishmash of magic and the promise of happily-ever-afters.

He disappears into the night like a dream you wake up from, but you're unsure if it was real or imagined. Needing to steady myself before returning to the cottage, I stare up at the moon. It remains the only permanent truth in my life. Dependable. Reliable. Present.

A far-off howl cries out in the night. Immediately I think of Alaric, but that would be impossible. The next full moon is a month away. It must be a coyote or wild dog.

Exhaustion overtakes me. I'm so tired I don't know if I can stand.

"Gi, are you coming?" Scott calls out again.

"On my way," I mumble, but I haven't the strength to continue walking. Instead, I fall to my knees, then stretch out on the ground. Heavy weights attach to my eyelids, and I'm much too tired to fight to keep them open.

Another howl fills the night. As much as I'd like to explain away the source of it, there's only one explanation that fits, and that is a truth I am not willing to acknowledge.

Denial provides a much more comfortable living space.

8

OTHERWORLDLY PICNIC

*E*xhaustion tore me from the world of the living and flung me into a near-unconscious state after Breas left. I only made it to my bed because Scott came out for me and found me curled up in a tight ball beside the new crescent moon garden I made for the nightlock. If not for him, I would have slept there all night, succumbing to exhaustion.

I remember Granda asking Scott if I was okay, and I tried to answer that I was, but it came out something like, "I'm ffff . . ." Then my tongue lost the ability to move.

Clarissa made some noise that resembled disappointment. She mentioned lessons, and I couldn't believe that she wanted to discuss our schooling with me almost asleep. Fortunately for her, I was too wiped out to argue. She was lucky my tongue went to sleep before the rest of me did.

I passed out as soon as Scott laid me on my bed. I was hoping for a dreamless sleep to last a hundred years, but morning came much too quickly. I know this because the damn tapestry that used to block the morning light was still missing, and the sun decided to burn my retinas with its brightness. If I was a vampire, I would be a flaming marshmallow.

Whoever stole it better enjoy their life while it lasts because if I get ahold of them, they'll discover the true meaning of pain. I may not be able to harm them with magic, but I've got other ways.

I shift around in my bed, attempting to avoid the light, but no matter where I hide, the brightness finds me, trying to brand me with its iron poke.

"Blast it." I finally fling off the blankets. No sleep for the wicked.

Nothing but strong black coffee doused with sugar will cure what's wrong with me. No magic-blocking herbs, just the kick in the ass I need to get through the day.

I stumble out into the kitchen and over to the coffee pot, only to find it empty.

"Heathens."

"Not everyone lives to serve you," Scott says.

I whirl around, ready to combat my nemesis with fists and legs. The early morning is no place for sarcasm, especially in the absence of caffeine. "If you don't want extreme force directed at your junk, you'd best be quiet until I get coffee into me."

He rolls his eyes and leans over the side of the chair to pick up a travel mug from the floor. "Here," he says, offering it to me. "I just wanted to mess with you. I forgot what a crank you are in the mornings."

"Cruel bastard," I growl, bringing the mug to my lips. The millisecond the hot liquid touches my tongue, my body immediately relaxes. The bitterness of Granda's blend still takes some time to get used to, but coffee is coffee. When I've had my fill for the time being, I cradle it in my hands.

"Better?"

"Much. Sorry the bitch came out to play."

He drinks from his own mug. I glance at the teapot on the table. The steeper is still in it. I still haven't told him the tea suppresses his magic. I will sometime, but he's had enough to deal with recently. He should be allowed to enjoy a small token of comfort and home. At least he knew to make me coffee instead.

"Where's Granda?"

"He left for the Cathedral. He said something about annals and seers, and I decided I didn't want to know what he was talking about."

"I hear that. Those dusty old volumes make me sneeze. They also make me cranky and make me want to break things."

He sips some more tea. "Gi, you always want to break things."

"True, but they make me want to cause a lot more damage than usual."

He smiles thoughtfully to himself. He missed "us." We ate breakfast at Gram's every morning of our lives. He's about to tell me as much and ask me if we can spend the day together when we're interrupted by someone knocking on the door.

His features harden as he walks over to it. "I wonder who that can be."

He assumes it's Alaric and is so preoccupied with the thought that he misses my reaction, which includes an ugly cry, a mild seizure, and a happy dance rolled into regret for missing the special dinner he had planned for me last night. I didn't even show up for dessert or let him know I wasn't coming. Instead I was a prisoner in my own home, forced to sit through dinner with a pompous prick. I mean, Breas did behave during the meal. He was quite charming actually, but for some reason everything gets fuzzy after that. I don't remember anything from the rest of the evening except for the dragging sleepiness once he left.

But it's not Alaric at the door. Scott's as startled as I am.

"Well, this is a surprise. I didn't think we'd see you again so soon," Scott says as he opens the door. In walks Breas with a giant basket, looking positively godlike in a snug T-shirt and just-as-snug jeans. A delicious piece of man-flesh, Lizzie would say. My middle tightens as I slip into the memory of our last kiss . . . weeks ago in the front yard of Gram's house for all the world to see. The same night he almost killed me on the motorcycle. My body, however, neglects to remember the almost-killed-me part and the way he left me after I refused to give in to him. If he wasn't staring at me now, I'd slap my face to pull myself together.

"I thought I'd invite Gigi to a breakfast picnic."

"Oh, that's nice," Scott says, but he doesn't think it's nice at all. He thinks this "surprise" picnic date was premeditated by one or both of us, and it's ruining his plans to hang out with me all day.

"Gigi, would you do me the honor of going on a picnic with me?"

I cross my arms to remind my body that Breas and I are not a couple. "I'm good, thanks."

"At least drink some of your coffee," he says, offering me a steaming cup. "Your favorite: hazelnut, espresso, cream, and just enough sugar to take off the bitterness."

Ireland provides many things, but I have yet to find the perfect combination of my favorite coffee. It's been weeks since I had a proper one. Weeks. I set my travel mug on the table, and my greedy little hands reach out and take it. My mouth waters as I lift the cup to my lips. And this time when the hot liquid hits my tongue, it's the most heavenly thing I ever drank. An angel made this delicious blend. An absolute angel, complete with shimmery white wings and a glowing halo.

Someone with more self-control would take their time to savor this heaven in a cup. I am not that person. I gulp it down in two swallows. Then I congratulate myself on my restraint—I wanted to do it in one.

As the wonderful beverage fills my belly and makes its way through my limbs and back to my heart, the anger and general hostility I feel every time Breas is around softens. Anyone who takes the effort to find me the perfect cup of coffee can't be all bad.

He winks at me as he lifts the basket in the air. "I've got another one in here."

My eyes widen and my lips smack together unconsciously. I am a slave to the bean.

He holds open the door for me. "After you."

Like a moth drawn to a flame just before its wings light up and disintegrate into ashes, I prowl out the door, already craving my next hit.

He reaches for my hand. Instinctively, I yank it away, but then, he whispers something before trying again, and this time I don't fight him. In fact, I can't figure out why I resisted him in the first place. He wants nothing more than to guide me on my journey.

He leads me past the gardens, past the pond, and to the fairy mound, releasing me only to drape a blanket across the ground. The moment we break contact, a vague sense of not wanting to be here with him tickles my mind. Like maybe it's wrong to be here with him.

Do not allow him to enter. It is what he wants.

He cradles my face in his hands. "You look a million miles away."

His touch pulls me back to the present.

"I'm right here."

He smiles at me. "As you should be."

A single thought emerges in my brain. *Should I?*

But I don't know if it's mine or Brigit's. I can feel the wrinkles in my forehead pinch together.

He reaches into the basket he brought and hands me a large travel mug. "Are you ready for your next cup?"

My lips smack together as I greedily reach for it. "Yes."

He pulls out a smaller basket with a towel folded over the top of it. "Scone? Fresh baked this morning."

Again, I accept what he has to offer. With my first bite I remember my first morning with . . . with . . .

Alaric. His name's Alaric.

Right. Alaric.

I stiffen. Alaric . . . I never went over to his house last night. He must be . . .

"Eat, Gigi, eat," Breas murmurs.

I take bite after bite while I drink the coffee. Whatever I was worried about disappears.

"That's it, Gigi," he whispers, but I can barely hear him. He sounds so far away, like he's underwater and I don't have enough strength to dive in and get him. Or I'm underwater, but too far away for him to get me.

He pulls out a book. A spell book. I think it might be the missing spell book from Vernal Falls. The one I found in Gram's attic. The one Lizzie got obsessed with. But it disappeared along with Kensey. I blink a few times, trying to focus, but everything's so blurry. I fight to keep awake, but that seems really hard too. Especially when I'm so very tired.

"You rest for now," he murmurs. "I'll wake you when I'm ready."

"M'kay," I think I say. The world shifts out of focus, and everything fades to black.

9

HOCUS-POCUS SPELLS OF THE MOSTUS

*S*cott found me at the fairy mound curled up in a ball around noon. When he asked where Breas was, I couldn't tell him because I didn't know. He either left me there or he was out exploring the countryside. When he returns and finds me gone, he'll know he messed up again. He's not gaining any points from Scott's point of view or mine.

I kneel down in front of the crescent moon garden to see how the nightlock seedlings are doing. Alaric and his welfare are never far from my mind. Yet Breas and I are connected too. Bound together as my vision suggests.

Me, a reincarnated goddess caught in a love triangle between two roguish Irish men. One, the direct descendent of the Original Werewolf who wants to kill me. The other, a once-upon-a-time asshole who suddenly turned Prince Charming, but instead of feeding me shiny red apples, he brings me chocolate biscuits, heavenly coffee, and clotted cream-capped scones with blackberry jam. Confusing for sure.

Scott kneels down beside me. "Why do you think he left you?"

I probe holes around the seedlings that have already begun to sprout. Nightlock is a fast-sowing seed. "I don't know."

"That was a major dick move. I really thought he was trying to impress you, but he abandoned you when you were sleeping. Anyone could have come along and grabbed you."

"Oh, Scott. Worried about the boogeyman in broad daylight?"

He layers in some mulch to help keep the ground moist. "Gi, I worry about you all the time. Especially now that we know you're a reincarnated goddess."

Why does he always need to bring that up? I still refuse to admit it to him, and he won't let it drop.

"Do we really need to go over this again? I'm just me. Just Gigi. But if you want to talk godly, what about you? Do you feel like a god?"

He stretches his arms out in front of him, almost hitting me. "I've always felt godly. Tall, muscular, athletic, classic good looks, lucky with the ladies."

"As if your ego wasn't already the size of a small country."

He pulls back into himself as if suddenly self-conscious. "You know I'm just kidding."

"Could have fooled me."

He sighs, "Gi, you know I'm not . . ."

Clarissa knocks our heads together. "Children, as you are already quite warmed up with intelligent banter, shall we begin your lessons?"

Scott's mouth hangs open. "Did you just conjure yourself here?"

"First lesson," she says, ambling down the path toward the fire pit, "always be on guard."

I follow behind her. "I'm suspicious by nature, and

therefore always on guard. Scott, however, is entirely too trusting."

He walks beside me. "Hey, I'm not too trusting. And might I point out, you didn't see her either."

I raise an eyebrow at him. "Clarissa, don't listen to him. He trusts people way too much—aside from boys that I like. Derg, the God of Death himself, could appear in front of him, and he would trust him."

Clarissa rests her hand on me. "That's actually a terrible example. Derg is your sibling as well as Oegden's. He may be the God of Death and capable of dastardly deals, but he is quite faithful to his brother in particular."

"See, Gigi, see?" Scott says, grinning from ear to ear.

"Great. Another fan of Team Scott. And why not his sister?"

"Well, she always liked to exert power over him to keep him from misbehaving. He often rebels."

"Brother rebellions. Fantastic. Can I expect another long-lost reincarnated brother to appear out of the ether as well?"

Clarissa rubs her hands together and a fireball appears. She guides it to the fire pit. "One can never say for certain, but oftentimes when a god appears on Earth, it is not in reincarnated form. It is in his or her full godly form."

I don't like where she's going with this conversation. I need to end it. "In case you weren't aware, I hate riddles. If you're trying to tell me something, just get to it."

She winks at me. "Fear not, Gigi. You've got everyone well in hand."

I look at Scott. "Why don't I like the sound of that?"

"Because you are a pessimist. I, on the other hand, am an optimist."

"If you'd been a freaky orphan most of your life, you might find yourself acting differently in these situations."

"Children, please! Amorin warned me about the incessant

talking the two of you are capable of, but there is a time and place, and now is neither one of those."

"Later," I whisper to Scott.

"Definitely," he replies.

She sweeps her left palm to the side as she mutters something. A large invisible hand covers my mouth, preventing me from saying another word. Scott seems to be wrestling with one over his mouth as well. His eyes take on that panicked look he gets when I've done something especially stupid and harmful to myself—which was often, growing up. It's disconcerting that I'm not the cause of it now.

"Children, I thought today we'd begin with something dramatic, just so you can see what your powers are capable of."

Scott swallows. The only magic he's experienced came from Carman's crazed Maleficium ambush. He's never witnessed the beauty of it. The powerful yet gentle energy that embraces everything and everyone in its path. He did throw that shield up against Alaric and Breas the other night, but he was so caught up in his anger, he didn't even know he was doing it. He couldn't appreciate his own ability. Now he seeks assurance that he and I will be okay.

I rest my hand on him. He instantly settles down.

"We will begin with fireball conjuring," Clarissa says and folds herself into a seated position. Scott and I do the same, sitting knee to knee with her.

According to Dad's journal, I started conjuring fireballs when I was four or five. It's the reason why Lizzie's parents left the coven and why they stopped allowing her to play with me. My first fireball conjuring episode also led Gram to give me my special tea, suppressing my magic—so no fireballs since then. And when I tried to form my own to fight Carman, my palms failed. Big time. I could only throw up a stupid shield—real exciting in battle.

"Rub your palms together," Clarissa says, and when she does, the invisible hands covering our mouths vanish.

We do as instructed.

"Focus," she whispers.

And I do. Heat begins to form in my palms. I rub harder and faster, and the heat continues to grow until, suddenly, a flame erupts in the middle.

"Teacher's pet," Scott snaps at me as he unsuccessfully tries to conjure his own.

"Focus on the rhythm of your palms," she says.

He follows her instructions exactly. His forehead wrinkles with the effort.

"I think a stick and rope would be faster," I whisper.

"Silence!" Clarissa shouts.

She's one tough broad. I wouldn't mess with her in a fireball fight. Luckily she's on our side. She dedicated her life to Brigit. She'll do anything to ensure my safety.

I practice making one after another. By the end, I barely need to rub my palms together and a fireball erupts. There's nothing to it once you know how—or at least for me. Scott doesn't seem to be able to make even a faint ember. I'm surprised he's having trouble. He's usually advanced in every situation. Thus, the inflated ego.

Clarissa calmly sits across from him. "Rub your palms."

He rubs them together.

"Good. Now envision a spark."

His forehead pinches.

"The heat you're generating between your hands provides the fuel."

He keeps rubbing and rubbing. "Nothing's happening," he sighs. Frustration pours out of him.

"Keep going. Picture that spark turning into a flame. It

keeps growing and growing until your hands can no longer contain it."

He tries again, and still nothing happens.

I glance at the fireball in my hands, then at Scott's empty ones. I want him to experience some success with Clarissa's lesson. I want him to believe in himself. I blow mine over to him.

"I did it! I did it!" he exclaims, his eyes open wide.

"You did! Great job!" I high-five him after he's tossed the fireball into the fire pit.

"Strange ways, the lot of you," Clarissa says.

"Welcome to our world. Can you teach me how to block my mind from people eavesdropping?"

Scott stops. "You can do that? You can keep Gigi out of your head?"

She shrugs. "It's not that difficult, but that will be a lesson for another day. Today, I'd like Scott to try a meditative visit to the Otherworld."

He gulps. "Am I ready for that?" He remembers the last time he and I tried to go on our own Otherworld visit. The night Gram died. The night he shot Ryan. He's nervous about what memories might surface and what, or who, he'll interact with.

"Gigi and I will be your guides."

I lay a hand on his arm. "Scott, you are woefully behind in your studies."

"On second thought, Gigi, don't you have a crescent moon garden to finish? Scott and I will take this first meditative journey together without your sisterly distraction."

"It's done. I'd like to come with you."

Gigi, Scott needs to learn how to journey on his own.

Why?

You won't always be around to guide him.

Where will I be?

Scott's head swings back and forth between us. He can't read our minds, but he knows we're talking about him. "Any chance we can verbalize this conversation?"

Clarissa clears her throat and looks me in the eye. "Do you mind if you and I speak later? Perhaps tomorrow. We have much to discuss."

Clarissa can see the future. If she says that he needs to go on without me, I guess he does. It must mean we will either get separated or my time with him will come to an end, and he needs to learn the tools to survive without me. I'd rather not think about what happens to me. I barely survived Samhain. Maybe I won't survive the coming storm. I don't know how I feel about that, but I guess there's nothing I can do about it.

"For today, I'll allow it, but I don't like it."

"Be well, Gigi," she calls out to me.

We're not through with this conversation.

Of course not, but Scott needs emotional cleansing. It'll be better for him if you're not there.

You're diabolical, using him.

I learned from the best.

"Ouch," I say to myself as I round the last bend of the garden. I approach the iron gate that forms a border between Granda's garden and the rest of the world. A raven watches me from the top of the gate. "She's direct. I'll give her that."

"Caw," he agrees.

Always someone with a comeback.

Left without Scott's supervision, I could have gone anywhere, done anything. I thought about going to Alaric's to apologize for missing dinner, but after my time with Breas, conflict swirls inside of me. Clarissa and Granda refuse to tell me anything about Breas. I wish that Dad was here to talk to. He'd know what to do, so do you want to know what I did? I spent the rest of the afternoon pouring over Dad's journal and a spell book I found under the floorboards in Granda's room—sue me for snooping. Evidently he and Gram like to stash books in similar hiding spots.

But after all my reading, I discovered he didn't record anything of consequence that Scott and I could use as a guide for our future. It's as if he suspected that I might read his diaries, searching for clues. He was a smart man.

The spell book, however, gives me an idea. One that will help me get the very thing I need to bring back everyone I love. And on the night of the Dark Moon, I'll find it.

10

VIOLENT DREAMS

"It's you," he snarls, fresh blood dripping from his canines. "You, who has kept me down for thousands of years. You, who tied my race to the powers of the moon. You, who made an immortal race mortal. I shall crush you and create an army that will never die. An army of immortal werewolves."

He smashes Scott's skull into the rock. Blood splatters across my face.

"No!" I scream. "No!"

"Gigi," someone murmurs into my ear. "Gigi, wake up!"

Danger breathes down my neck. The heat sears me in place. I know that I must fight for consciousness, even as it slips away again. Consumed with darkness, I shake my head back and forth to wake up. To rid myself of this dazed feeling. I take several long, deep breaths before I'm able to take in my surroundings. Rock circle to host a fire. Ashes where once there were hot coals. Magic performed in cauldron. In the air. All around me. Death. Chaos. Destruction. Carman. Her fire. Her flame. Her circle.

No longer constrained by ancient body.

No longer tied to this world.

"What am I doing here?" I whisper to myself thinking I'm alone but soon realizing I'm not.

Alaric stops on the other side of the circle, choosing the darkness of the night rather than the light cast from the fire. "I was just going to ask you the same thing."

There's accusation in his voice. Accusation that I've done something wrong. A faint memory of me doing something to upset him stirs within me. The reason remains dull and fuzzy. Unimportant with him here.

Anger swirls around him, reminding me of getting swept up in a tornado. So far as I know, we're not in Kansas. Or if we are, I need to enter into one of those sleep studies immediately.

"Did I do something wrong?"

An invisible force separates us. I try to move closer, but he backs away. "You can say that."

I reach out for him, silently calling him to me. He crosses his arms.

"What did I do? I don't even understand how I got here."

He must realize I'm telling the truth, because his stance loosens and he shifts closer.

"If Nan was around, I'd think you were summoned, but she's not here, or at least not showing herself. Her herbs and magical objects have disappeared, but she's also done that before."

That stops me. "She has?"

Clayone led me to believe Carman was dead or at least dying at her altar. It was me that assumed she died—I have no physical proof of it. I didn't ask Granda to provide me with an inventory of the dead or ask for a total body count. It was easier, it *is* easier, to believe that she's dead, but that doesn't explain why her things are missing. Dad warned me about the Fomorians, and how she was trying to summon them. I've no idea who or what the Fomorians are, but maybe Carman's story isn't finished yet.

Maybe she isn't dead.

And that would mean that a psycho revenge-bent witch ready to kill me at the next opportunity is on the run, planning her next evil plan. Clarissa said I won't always be there for Scott. Now I know why.

"I already told you that she often leaves for long stretches of time to meditate or do magic or something, or did you feign interest in that as much as you feigned interest in me?" The hurt in his voice stabs me between the eyes.

"Feign interest? I don't know what you're talking about. I'm interested in you."

He curls his hands into fists. His green eyes flash in the darkness. "Are you sure? Because I saw you curled up in that bastard's arms more than once."

The full realization of what I did the night before and earlier today hits me. I remember everything. "Breas. You mean Breas."

"You kissed him with as much passion as you kiss me. Maybe more."

Suddenly, it hits me. Granted sometimes it takes me a while, but eventually I'll get there. "It was you in the darkness watching us, wasn't it."

He lifts his chin. He'll not be made to feel a coward. "What if it was?"

"You were stalking me."

"I wasn't stalking you. I was watching out for you. He almost killed you on the motorcycle and left you for dead, and still you kissed him the way you kissed me."

Breas reaching down to kiss me. My lips finding his. My arms slipping around his neck to pull him closer. He speaks the truth, but still I resist the truth of my actions. "I didn't."

"You did."

Confusion plagues me. Alaric consumes my mind and heart, so why did I kiss Breas?

Because I am an asshole. An absolute fucking asshole. Defeat settles over me. It's not a feeling I'm entirely comfortable with, though I'm completely familiar with it. Truth spills out of me like vomit. "I don't know what came over me. I wasn't myself. I wasn't in control of my own emotions or actions."

He edges closer and inhales deeply. "I know what happened. I smell the magic on you still."

"You think I was spelled?"

"I know you were."

It would make sense. Especially when I typically think Breas is a jerk, and then I hook up with him.

As the tension leaves Alaric's body, it seems that he's forgiven me for my slip. Now it's my turn to push him to his own truth reveal. "How can you smell it, Alaric?"

He turns away from me. "I just can."

"That's not an answer, and you know it."

"It's the truth."

I step toward him. Conflict swirls around him. Though I can't read his mind, I know he wants to tell me. He's just afraid to. "How, Alaric? How? Why can't you tell me?"

"I think you know why," he whispers.

I catch my breath. It's the closest we've come to the truth, and I'm scared shitless.

He breaks through the weak shield I must have thrown up as we approach his confession and steps up to me. "Is that why you turned to him?"

I whisper much quieter than I intended, "Was it you howling in the distance?"

"You know the answer."

I suck in air because the world grows fuzzy around me

and getting oxygen into my lungs seems like a really smart idea.

He hovers over me, waiting for me to admit what I know. Admit the truth. When I don't respond, his muscles tense. "Say it, Gigi. Say it."

The magic blanket Breas laid upon me lifts, and suddenly, I know everything. I see everything.

"You're a werewolf."

His green eyes flash in the darkness. "Are you scared?"

My heart skips a beat but not for the reason he suggested. "No."

He laughs, a sad, deep, mocking laugh as he distances himself from me. "You should be."

I rush over to him, pulling him into me. "You're not capable of hurting me."

He tries to break away, but I'm surprisingly strong, or his efforts are especially half-assed. "I'm capable of killing you."

I pull him closer. My crystal necklace presses into my chest, but not in a painful way, more as a promise that Alaric and I will work it out. "You won't."

"How do you know?"

"I just do."

"That's not a good enough answer."

"Because we've been together before."

"Before as in Vernal Falls?"

"Before that."

His forehead furrows in that way I find absolutely adorable. "I don't understand."

"I think you do."

He closes his eyes and pictures us together. I may not be able to read his mind, but I can tell what he's thinking. "In another life," he says in a small, quiet voice.

"Yes."

He staggers backward. "How do I even know that? How is that even possible?"

How is it possible that he's a werewolf? How's it possible I'm a reincarnated goddess? I don't freaking know how any of it is possible. He needs time to process everything. To build on what I've told him.

He struggles to comprehend. "But I'm a werewolf."

"In this life."

A question pervades the space between us. A sharp intake of breath. A hesitation. A concern, but also a pressing need to know. "Was I a werewolf in my other one?"

Gram talked about past-life regressions. She even had a friend, Jim Ayers, who would come over and they'd do regressions with a group of friends I now know were part of her coven. She never talked about her past lives or what she learned. Scott and I used to watch from between the spindles of the banister, only occasionally getting caught. We'd sit up there while he talked the person into a deep sleep, constantly beckoning them toward a stone cottage with a bright light. From there they'd venture to wherever the person lived in another life. I remember the way the heaviness fell over me and the way it weighed down on my eyelids when one of them slipped under.

I close my eyes and let thoughts and feelings wash over me. I acknowledge the ones that are not related to Alaric and honor those that are. I allow warmth and light to sweep into me and through me, soon shifting into premonitions. I know I reincarnated as Brigit of Kildare, but there have been other reincarnations. A coast. An ocean. A boat. Alaric. Me.

Lost at sea.

Drowned to stop himself from killing me.

Tell him the truth of my visions?

I can't.

I won't.

Instead I press my lips to his. We drown ourselves in each other. The image of him swimming out to sea. First as a man. Then as a wolf. Swimming out to the middle of the ocean. Waiting for death to take him.

Me, walking alone on the beach. Wondering where he disappeared to. Longing for him. Abandoned. Confused. Destroyed. Stay or go? Not wanting to be parted from him. Tears streaming down my face. Sadness consuming me. Allowing the sea to take me. Shedding the mortal human form for the immortal one.

He pulls away, still cradling me in his arms. "What do you see?"

"I see us together."

He presses his forehead to mine. "As it should be."

For now. For this moment. I soak it in. Because sometimes we only have today. My crystal necklace shares the space between us, and it gives me an idea—a way to ensure Alaric remains with me as a man and not as a wolf.

Scott kneels beside me on his own kneepad in front of the crescent moon garden. I spend most of my time working on it. "Where do you keep disappearing to?"

Evidently he searched for me this morning. If he knew I sleepwalked all the way to the remains of Carman's bonfire and Alaric found me there, he'd go more Ultimate Protector than he already is. He'd probably block off my window from the outside and add a lock to my door to prevent me from escaping, or take to standing guard while I slept. "Trust me. You don't want to know."

"Gi, I do. I want to be a part of your life. We're strangers here."

His sadness seeps into my soul. "Scott, we're not strangers. We will never be strangers."

"Then why do I feel like you're only sharing half of your life with me? Half of you?"

My shoulders round in on themselves. "When Lizzie died, then Ryan, parts of me died too. I'd do anything to bring them back."

"Gi, they're dead. They're not coming back."

"What if I told you they could?"

"Defies the natural law, but go on."

"Brigit once possessed the Vessel of Life. She could bring people back from the dead."

"Is that what you used on me?"

Most of the night of Samhain remains a mystery to him. He hasn't asked, and I haven't told him how he survived or how Dad and Calliope didn't.

"No, that was the Chalice of Healing. And that disappeared with the cows. The Vessel of Life can bring back the dead, but it's been missing for thousands of years."

"And you think that if you find it you can bring Lizzie and Ryan back from the dead?"

I reach for his hand. "I think I can bring them all back."

Hope blossoms along with a heavy dose of skepticism. He purses his lips. "You mean Dad and Mom?"

"I mean Dad, Calliope, Gram, everyone."

"Gi, I don't know much about magic and life-force, but I believe that nothing can be given without something taken away."

He holds no memories of his past lives or his immortal one aside from what Granda told him the night he killed Ryan. He doesn't know about the alleged rules of the Vessel of Life. The one about a soul splitting when returned. If he knew that one, he'd stop this conversation before we even really dug in. But what he doesn't know won't kill him.

"But what if, with the Vessel of Life, none of those rules

apply? After all, it's a tool created by the gods. Why would a god create a tool that would require such sacrifice?"

"It's not worth the risk." His mind shuts off. I haven't convinced him. Not yet anyway.

"If your dreams don't scare you, they're not big enough." I pass off the quote from a keychain I used to carry around on my backpack as my own. Let him believe it's goddessy wisdom.

"What if your nightmares scare the shit out of you? Are you willing to risk your life for them? For your soul?"

So he does know, or at least he's equating Voldemort's soul splitting into Horcruxes with the Vessel of Life. Same difference really. "You know I would."

"But, Gigi, it's your soul we're talking about. Your soul."

"And I'd trade it for the ones I love."

"You don't realize the full impact of what you're suggesting."

There he goes, assuming I haven't thought through all aspects of this. Still believing that there's a good side to me. But he's wrong. He's always been wrong. A goddess who requires such high sacrifice for her survival cannot be someone of consequence.

"I do, and nothing will stop me from acquiring it." The makings of a spell I read the night I found the spell book in Gram's attic along with the spells I found last night take shape in my mind. "Will you help me?"

Conflict and distrust exude from him. "What do you have in mind?"

"Remember the scene from *Clash of the Titans* with the three witches and the one eyeball that gave them sight?"

The color seeps out of his already pale cheeks. He had nightmares for weeks, maybe months, after we first watched the movie. He caught me watching the scene one time when he was supposed to be at practice. The next time I tried to watch it, the DVD was gone. His face pinches at the memory.

I wink at him, a smirk creeping across my face. "It'll be nothing like that."

The tension leaves his body and his shield drops—I know I've got him. Lured him in with a false sense of calm. Pretend to feed him his worst nightmare then hand him a promising morsel instead.

"When will you be conducting this 'magical' vessel-finding spell?"

"At the Dark Moon."

Nervous energy radiates off him. "Are you going to ask Granda or Clarissa for assistance?"

"I don't think they'd be too willing to help me."

"But you knew I would be."

"Great minds . . ."

"We don't think alike, Gigi. Definitely not thinking alike on this one."

"We'll see about that." I pat his arm to reassure him. To him, he thinks it's just an innocent pat from his sister. In actuality, I'm transferring positive, calm energy to him. He needs to be there to help me at the Dark Moon. I can't work the spell without him to ground me. Scott isn't just vital to my existence as Gigi Brennan, he is also vital to my existence as Brigit. He extends my magic.

"At least I have a couple weeks to make you change your mind."

"You know I'm a stubborn one."

He wraps his arm around me. He suspects I'm the reason behind his newfound calmness, but he decides not to mention it.

"Gigi, you've been stubborn since the day you were born."

"Thank you."

"A fierce, stubborn pain in the ass."

"You're so kind."

"An outrageously self-centered, fierce, stubborn pain in the ass."

"I get the picture.

"A—"

I jab him in the stomach. "Now's not the time to use every adjective you've ever learned in a sentence."

He smiles, pulling away from me. "I feel like it's always the time, and you give me so much to work with . . ."

11

HIT THE PUB

The night belongs to the brave. Or the curious. Or the mostly stupid. That's probably why I loved sneaking out so much back in Vernal Falls.

It began as prowling around the neighborhood. Testing the reach of outdoor motion lights before they went off. Discovering who locked their doors at night and who didn't. Finding out who owned dogs and how friendly they were to strangers.

When the thrills of nightly escapades into backyards grew uninspiring, Pittsburgh's streets and clubs became my new playground. Every trip proved thrilling, and sometimes scary as shit, but it always pushed the boundaries of living on the edge.

Since arriving in Ireland, my adventures have revolved around evil Maleficium sorcerers and four-legged Original Werewolves. A night of debauchery at the local club would be a welcome change, and I suggested as much to Scott, especially after his meditative Otherworld trip with Clarissa. He managed to expel some of his negative emotions, but he's still holding onto extra layers out of habit.

"A club?" he says, staring at me as if I had grown a third eye.

"A club," I repeat after him. "You need some fun."

"Fun?" He echoes me as if he's never heard the concept before.

"Yes, fun. You know, get out, socialize, dance, kiss some people, with any luck get inappropriately groped and smash them in the vitals."

"And this is fun to you?"

"Well, maybe not the inappropriately groped part, but in the right setting . . . sure, why not?"

Scott needs to get out. Since Ryan's death, he's moved from one imprisonment to the next. First juvie, where his own guilt bound him to the locked cell more than physical shackles ever could. Then his mom bound him to a room where he was forced to hear me feet away from him but was unable to make me aware of his presence. Then magically tortured by Carman. Then forced to witness the death of his mom and dad before almost dying himself and only surviving by drinking the spelled blood of his sister who happens to be a reincarnated goddess. And now, forced to live in a strange land without his closest loved ones (other than me, of course) and his best friends—it's a lot.

He accused me of being removed from him. I suppose that's true. And I want to make it up to him.

"To a club."

"Yes."

"Me and you?"

"Yes, me and you. It'll be a positive brother-sister bonding experience for us. You know, where we can spend time together without getting threatened with death or tortured or manipulated in some way."

"Only the two of us?" he asks with an unmistakable dash of skepticism.

"Yep, just the two of us."

"No one else will be there?"

"Well, I can't guarantee we'll be alone—it's a public place with a band. There's bound to be some fans."

Alaric's band, Run with Silver, will be playing, but Scott doesn't need to know that. I've got to get him to agree to go out with me first before I share other tidbits of information. Besides, Alaric will be onstage performing, and not sucking out my tonsils until at least the second half of the night.

"I'll go, provided we leave when I want to, and no ditching me."

I pull my hands into my chest, aghast. "I'd never."

"You absolutely would."

I'd like to argue with him, but the burn in my throat makes it impossible to talk. Must be that lying to brothers is worse than lying to nonrelations. An unfortunate by-product of a conscience, but one I'll work through. "Agreed."

If Granda was surprised we were hitting the town of Kildare, he didn't show it aside from a twinkle in his eye, but I think that was more about him being happy for us "living" than surprise. I keep trying to read his mind because now it's like a challenge, and I've never been one to turn down a dare, but his mind is completely closed off to me. I really need to learn how he does that.

Scott stops in front of the door to Hell's Gate. "How did you find this place?"

I wink at him. "How do I find any place of mischief?"

"You're drawn to it like honey."

"Cliché, but true."

The darkness of the interior envelops us as we enter. A thick haze of energy wafts over. I take a deep breath and suck it in. I'm becoming aware of the different types of energy and their power and purpose. Scott latches onto the back of my shirt. "Stay close," he whispers. "I don't want to lose you."

I wind my way through the crowd to the bar. I flash two fingers at the bartender, and she pours us two pints. Scott pays her, because that's the type of guy he is, then he reattaches himself to my shirt and I find an open table in front of the stage.

After we sit, we knock our glasses together in celebration. The beer tastes thick and rich, far different than the crap served back in the States. Not that I'm a true connoisseur of beer or anything, but everything tastes better in Ireland. Even the air.

"How do you manage to get served everywhere you go?"

"I'm very convincing."

He shifts closer so he doesn't have to shout. "You are, aren't you."

"So are you."

"I always thought it was because of my charming, sparkly personality," he glances around to make sure no one's listening. With the growing crowd, he's got nothing to worry about. "Now I think I compel people to do what I want. Is that even possible?"

"It's magic."

"Magic," he repeats.

"Or a gift."

Negativity courses through his brain. "Or a curse . . . How do I know a person does something for me because they want to and not because I talked them into it?"

"Trust that you use it only when necessary."

He thinks about all the girls he's dated—and he'd dated a lot of them—and the way many of them, especially the ones this past year threw themselves at him. He worries that he persuaded them to hook up with him rather than them actually wanting to. "But how will I know?"

"You will. It's like a switch you turn on and off."

An image of him persuading Principal Donahue to go up to the school attic to investigate an old mascot costume rather than adding another year onto my disciplinary sentence flashes through his brain.

"Yep, exactly. You turned it on."

He rests his hand over mine. "How much of my mind can you read?"

We've never discussed the exact nature of how we communicate with each other. It's unfamiliar territory, admitting our freakishness to one another aloud. "Do you really want to know?"

He takes a long drag of his pint, his mind spiraling through all the different scenarios. He settles on the suspected truth but wants to say it aloud. "You can read all of it, can't you."

I nod in confirmation.

"Is there a way to turn if off or block you?"

"Worried about what I might find?"

"No, just wondering why you couldn't read my mind when I was in the barn at the psycho witch's place." He remembers the dark room with the chains and traps hanging on the walls and the sound of me calling out for Carman and him not being able to yell out to me.

"I couldn't read anyone after Ryan died until Samhain when Carman revealed her intentions with you."

"Why is that, do you think?"

"I've wondered that myself. Maybe you give me power? I also stopped drinking Gram's tea, thinking maybe that's why I couldn't read anyone's mind, though I could do it back home when I was drinking her tea all the time."

He takes another sip of his beer. "It suppresses magic, doesn't it."

"Yes," I whisper, suddenly feeling very guilty even though I didn't tell him for his own good. "I should have told you."

He shrugs. "I already knew, or at least suspected it. In juvie I had surges of power. Like I could break the door if I really wanted to or flick it open with my wrist. When Mom showed up, she did something to me and I lost it. I thought maybe the strength came from my grief, but now I know she spelled me to suppress it. I don't know if it was to protect me or to protect her. Based on past actions, probably her."

Sadness falls over him again. I can't let it swallow him whole. I settle for distraction. "The night Alaric and Breas fought, you seemed really strong and fast."

He winks at me. "I am very strong and fast."

"Ego trip much?"

He laughs. I laugh along with him. It's the first time we've laughed together since . . .

We both sober up immediately, remembering the campfire with Lizzie and Ryan. The night before everything went to shit.

"I miss them," I sigh.

He picks up my empty glass. "Me too. Let's drink ourselves into oblivion."

"Sounds like a brilliant plan."

Scott may act more like a Boy Scout than an adrenaline-seeking rebel the majority of the time, but he can party with the best of them when he's in the mood, and he's definitely in the mood.

After all the crap we've gone through, I am too.

Declan and Madigan take the stage first. Madigan's the drummer, and Declan picks up the bass guitar. A few of the other bandmates walk in front of an instrument or microphone. They start playing loud and fast, just the way I like it.

"And now for the lead singer of Run with Silver . . ."

A single light flashes on Alaric who somehow appeared without anyone noticing him, including me. His black leather jacket and ripped jeans with kick-ass motorcycle boots make him so freaking sexy. My god, he is a god.

"You neglected to mention that Alaric was performing tonight."

I'd have to be completely intoxicated to miss the waves of accusation. "Did I?"

"I thought it was just going to be the two of us. You know, brother-sister bonding time."

"We are bonding. He's onstage. You're here with me."

"Hmmm," he grumbles.

"Come on. Lighten up. Finish your pint."

And he does as he's told. "I will return," he promises, our empties in hand. "Perhaps I'll return with a shot of something, just to keep things interesting."

"I always liked you," I wink at him.

"Flattery will get you nowhere, my dear sister. I'm still mad at you for tricking me into watching your boyfriend's band."

"Admit it. You love getting out into the world and being around the young and the stupid."

"You're certainly stupid all right," he knocks into my shoulder before heading to the bar.

With him occupied, I finally turn my attention to Alaric and his band. The moment my eyes find him, he winks at me as if he's been watching me the entire time and waiting for me to look at him. Seeing him onstage makes me want him more.

Something binds us together, but not in the same way the ribbon joined Breas and me. I didn't have a choice in that binding. It was to serve a purpose, a joined cause, but it wasn't permanent. Alaric disappeared from at least one of my past lives but not in the way Breas did. He didn't want to hurt me.

Breas wanted something. Wanted to take something that wasn't his. Anger blasts from me. My palms burn with fire. I clasp them together to contain the energy that wants to escape before glancing around to make sure no one witnessed my little witchy display. Luckily everyone's mind is occupied with Run with Silver. More than a few of the women are thinking about what they'd like to do with Alaric. Green energy tickles my nose. How predictable that jealousy appears green. I blink the thought away. It is an energy-depleting emotion.

Alaric picked me. He seeks me out. He wants me. And now his voice lures me to the dance floor. I can barely contain myself. If Scott doesn't get here soon, I'll have no choice but to break my promise and lose myself to the music.

When my brother doesn't return in an acceptable time, and my patience can't wait a second longer, I search the bar, curious to find out what's taking him so long. I find him in the far corner, talking to some brunette. I close my eyes and dial in on his mind. She's pretty and vaguely familiar. She reminds me of one of the football groupies. That's what Scott's thinking too. He likes talking to her, but he feels bad about leaving me alone. After all, he's the one who accused me of ditching him, and now he's the one doing it to me.

Bring her over.

His eyes meet mine.

You sure?

Totally.

He asks her if she'd like to come over with him. She agrees and follows behind him as he makes his way back over to me. He hands me a pint and hands the other one to her. "Gigi, I'd like you to meet Maria. Maria, this is my sister, Gigi. You two get to know each other. I'll be right back," he says and disappears to buy another pint.

I curse him for leaving me with a stranger. He knows I

hate awkward conversations with people I don't know. I don't always like conversations with people I do know.

I take a stab at reading her mind, but it's foggy, densely populated with conflicting thoughts and emotions as if someone is screaming to get out and someone else is bashing her down.

She smiles at me like she's letting me in on a giant secret. "So, Gigi, Scott tells me you're from Vernal Falls."

I will make sure he dies a miserable, torturous death. I might not be able to magic him, but I can shove slivers of wood into his eyeballs.

While I think about all the ways to make Scott pay for leaving me with this stranger, I play the perfect conversationalist. "Born and raised."

"And how do you like Kildare?"

I stare up at Alaric, trying not to push my thoughts into him about taking a break, but I'd really like him to take one. Especially now, since Scott found a friend. "It's been interesting."

"I'm sure. Kildare is a magical place."

I try probing her mind again to figure out what she means by "magical," but Scott steps between us. He can't tell if I'm trying to read her mind or not, but he doesn't want me intruding on someone else's thoughts without their permission. Especially someone he thinks is hot.

Fabulous. He's back to his annoying conscientious self.

"Did my sister keep you entertained, Maria?"

"I believe it is I who should have amused her. You two are new to Kildare. I've lived here all my life."

They fall into an easy conversation about her life in Kildare versus his life in Vernal Falls. He keeps thinking how luscious her lips look and how he'd like to kiss her.

And that's my signal to get out of his head before his

thoughts become more amorous. My attention wanders back to the stage.

The rhythm of the beat makes my feet move on their own. My body soon follows. The music wants to take me away from Scott and Maria, and I let it. I won't be joined by a mysterious dance partner tonight because he's the one drawing me onto the dance floor. And that's okay. I'll dance for him, and he will want me more.

My shirt slips off my shoulder, revealing the never-ending triskele tattoo. I leave it exposed. Alaric hasn't seen any of my tattoos yet. We've been interrupted every time we've tried to get closer, and I figure he might like a little looksie. Maybe it'll help encourage him to take a break even though he just began. He's probably got tattoos of his own, and I'd like any excuse to see them.

The hair on the back of my neck stands up. I look over at Declan. He's staring at me. Without thinking, I zone in on his mind, but at the last minute I decide against it. His aggression when we first met pales in comparison to the vicious glare he's giving me now. If laser beams could shoot out of his eyes, I'd be in big trouble. I adjust my shirt to cover the tattoo, and immediately his attention shifts away. I need to stay away from him. He's dangerous. When we first met, he drew my name out of me without me even realizing what was going on. Now I realize he compelled me to speak.

Is he magical or a werewolf too?

The music shifts from fast to faster and sweeps me away with it. Suddenly nothing else matters. Scott and Maria join me on the dance floor. They're moving to a much different rhythm than what Alaric's performing on the stage, but that has more to do with alcohol and hormones—an exotic combination, given the right circumstances. I keep up with him though. He won't lose me to his music.

I let myself fall into his beat, closing my mind off to the

thought signatures of Scott, Maria who's still foggy, and the random strangers in the room who I could care less about. I seek escape above all else. The thick beer, the sultry energy buzzing all around me, and Alaric's music spread out through my limbs, easing every nerve, soothing every worry, relaxing me to my very core. After weeks with little reprieve loaded with misery, my eyes slide shut and the music takes me somewhere else. A place where Alaric and I can be together without the complications of him being a werewolf and me being a reincarnated goddess. There, we are just us.

Static energy crackles around me, rattling my mind back to the room full of people. Something's familiar. A mind I've known before. All my life, in fact, but gone. Erased from this plane.

Not erased.

Not gone.

Summoned.

Lizzie.

She's here. I can feel her.

I spread out my mind to reach for her, her signature as familiar to me as Scott's. It should be easy to find her. Much faster than searching through the throngs of people. When my search doesn't find her, I send out a plea.

Please, Lizzie, please.

Reveal yourself.

But my plea goes unanswered.

No longer willing to wait for her to come to me, I cut in and out of the crowd, pulling bodies apart just to make sure she's not dancing with someone nearby and ignoring my call.

An intense pressure squeezes my throat. A force rivaling my own tries to cut off my airway. I murmur a counter spell, ridding evildoers from harming me or anyone in the room, because suddenly it strikes me—I can protect the people around me. As I glance around to find the person hexing me,

Maria gives me a tight nod, but I know it can't be her. She and Scott are wrapped together tighter than a caterpillar in a cocoon. Declan?

I search the stage for the bassist. He's nowhere to be seen. Maybe it was him who tried to curse me, but only a powerful witch could curse someone without being present. A witch like Carman or Calliope, and they're both dead. Or supposed to be. Now I'm not so sure. These "rules" for magic and Druidry and reincarnated gods and goddesses are new to me and change everything.

Declan reappears a second later from behind the curtain. I rule him out immediately.

Then who?

Not who. What.

What? What do you mean, what?

You know.

If you assumed that listening to the voices in your head would lead to moments of clarity, especially when that voice is from a goddess, you would be mistaken. Brigit never learned the importance of specificity.

A wolf much different than the one Alaric conjured at the well appears in my mind.

A wolf then.

Familiar with Alaric's "mind channel," I search for one similar but not his. Four bandmates onstage broadcast that same fuzziness of his. I stretch my mind across the dance floor again, but this time, it's like they're all wolves. Like a wolf army has descended on the room. But not one is in wolf form.

I close my eyes again and let my thoughts take me. She's here. It is Lizzie. In ghost form?

No.

Summoned.

There's that summoned thought again. I feel someone

probe my mind. I spin back to the stage. The curtains behind Madigan shift and bunch. I take off in chase but am abruptly pulled back by a meaty hook.

"The luck of the Irish is upon us!" Breas squeezes me into his chest.

I shove my fist into him and extract myself from his tentacles. "Keep your hands to yourself."

"Oh, Gigi. I thought we came so far the other day."

Scott rushes over with Maria close by his side. I force myself between them. "And now we are an ocean apart."

"We have been an ocean apart before, and still it has not separated us, but no matter. We've got time. Plenty of it. And you are?" He offers a hand to Maria. She tentatively reaches hers out, and he kisses it.

She swallows, obviously uncomfortable with a stranger kissing her appendage, even if he is gorgeous. "Maria."

"Have we met?"

She removes her hand and entwines it with Scott's. "I don't think so. I don't get out much."

"I haven't been out for a very long time," he offers. "No matter. Tonight's for the wicked. Scott, Gigi, you remember Kensey?"

My mouth unhinges and smashes to the floor. "Kensey?"

She looks over at me, but there's no recollection in her eyes. She acts like she doesn't know who I am, and she most definitely does know me. I've got a decade worth of angsty journal pages to prove it.

"What's wrong with you?"

She blinks and her pupils shift back into place. "It's you."

"Nice to see you too."

"Is your little wolfie friend around?"

Does she know something I don't? Panic rises within me, but I push it down. She doesn't know. It's just Kensey being Kensey. "And who might you be referring to?"

"Your bestie who follows you around like a love-sick puppy. Always looking for a handout. Always protecting you when you make a mistake. Always around."

"You mean Lizzie."

"Yeah, I do. How did you manage to come to Ireland without her? I didn't think you two ever parted. How did you get her to leave your side? Did she finally realize what a skank whore you are?"

"For one, she's dead."

"Dead," she whispers, almost sounding like she's sorry. Then she remembers Lizzie trying to curse her in the school hallway and her spell work in the attic, and she's not the least bit upset. In fact, she's downright glad it happened. The bitch.

"What are you doing here?" I snarl at her. I may not be a werewolf, but she's really working my hackles.

"Oh, Breas," she says, looping her arm through his. "He and I are in love."

He's been in Ireland with Kensey while he's been courting me. Is she the reason he abandoned me at the fairy mound? So much for Prince Charming. He poisons everything he touches. I will not fall under his spell again.

"Is that so?" I ask her but look at Breas. "I was under the impression that he was interested in someone else."

"Oh, Gigi. Subtle wordplay does not become you," he says. "It is true that I brought Kensey with me, but you know I want you too."

"Oh, so the three of us will be a happy threesome together?"

He slides over and tries to drape an arm over me, but I move away from him.

"You, me, Kensey, what could be more pleasurable?"

"I can think of a number of things."

Midsong the music stops. The crowd instantly goes silent.

Alaric leaps off the stage, landing feet away from us. He cleared almost twenty-five feet.

Scott begins pushing Breas toward the door. "Breas, I think that's your signal to leave."

"But I've not convinced her yet."

"She's not interested in joining your harem."

"Are you sure about that?" he says, loud enough for me to hear.

Scott keeps pushing him. "Quite. Now go."

Maria stands beside me. "It appears that you're in demand."

"What did he want?" Alaric growls, rushing past me.

I manage to grab him before he takes off through the crowd. "Nothing. Scott handled it."

He tugs me along. "I told him if he touched you again that I was going to kill him, and look at everything he's done to you since then. It's time to deliver on that promise."

His anger clears his mind. All he can think about is Breas kissing me, and then the discovery at the site of Carman's bonfire that I was spelled. He wants to tear him apart. I'm half-tempted to let him.

"Alaric, he's not worth it. Trust me. Of all the mistakes I've made, I can confirm that he is not worth the energy."

He keeps pulling me along.

"Alaric, please don't."

Scott blocks his path. "And where do you think you're going?"

"To kill him."

"Oh," he laughs, "you Irish are dramatic. I'll give you that. There won't be bloodshed tonight if I can help it. Tomorrow, well, that's another day. Now, pay attention to my sister or I'll be forced to rid this establishment of you."

Alaric stares at him. His fists still tight. "I'd like to see you try."

Scott laughs, blowing him off. He's not intimidated in the least. Me? I'm scared shitless. I mean, I might be able to shoot fireballs out my hands to light a campfire, but if Alaric and Scott go to blows, I don't think I'll be able to stop them.

Scott steps into Alaric's personal space. Tension crackles between them.

Breathe, Brigit whispers.

And I do. Then focus calming energy on the two of them, imagining a blanket that wraps each of them into a snuggly cocoon and keeps them safe.

Soon the aggression dies, replaced by something else—euphoria I think—and I realize I might have overdone it. Scott turns to Maria, and Alaric takes me in his arms. He lifts me up in the air, his eyes twinkling. I try to reduce their excitement down to an acceptable club level, but I can't concentrate with his touch.

"You're coming with me." Alaric laughs as he carries me back to the stage, and the entire club laughs along with him.

I think I might have underestimated my power, or the beers loosened my focus. I'll need to either change my ways or learn how to funnel my power instead of broadcasting it, but I guess there's really no harm in a place full of happy people.

He sits me down on a speaker. "Now I won't lose you in the crowd or have you carted off by some asshole."

"Possessive much?"

His nostrils flare. "Yes. You're mine."

Anger boils in my veins. I won't argue with him here, but he needs to learn that I, Gigi Brennan, belong to no one.

DRUNKEN MEANDERINGS

*A*laric's claiming of me almost ruined my night. I was also upset I never found Lizzie at the club—Breas screwed that one up. Eventually, the music and the hyped-up energy of the crowd wore me down, or softened me—I'm not sure which—but either way as the night wore on I didn't feel so angry and mistreated anymore.

It was around that same time that Scott began delivering beers, to me first, and then to Alaric and the other band members. He'd "sneak" across the stage on tiptoe with a stupid-ass grin and deliver a half-empty pint because he either drank most of it or spilled it along the way. He'd curtsy to the crowd once he successfully delivered the beer. They'd congratulate him with whistles and cheers. He'd bashfully wave his hand at them in an "aw shucks" way before sneaking back across the stage, always managing to walk in front of Alaric. Alaric was good natured about it. He didn't go all diva at Scott for taking away from his performance. Actually, he seemed to enjoy the diversion. The first time, he shook his head, silently laughing at him as he sang. Soon after, they began verbally exchanging greetings and thank yous and what's ups. Then the fist bumps started —their friendship accelerating at a rapid pace. When the two embraced, the crowd went wild.

When Scott wasn't delivering drinks or polishing off his own, he spent his time dirty dancing with Maria, leading more with his boy parts than his brain, which was very unlike him, but Maria didn't seem to mind. She just kept dancing with him, only stopping when he left for another pint, which was quite often. It was at those moments when she interested me the most. He'd leave for the bar, and she'd stop moving. She didn't even sway to the music even though everyone around her was dancing. She acted as if it was the very last thing she wanted to be doing with her time, but as soon as Scott returned, she'd take the drink offered—if there was one—and start dancing again. It was all very methodical and didn't sit right with me at all.

Don't get me wrong. Scott was happy, and that's all I wanted for him tonight, but something seemed off with Maria, and I was determined to find out what.

I tried reading her again, sending out signals but getting nothing. Nada. Zip. Not even the impressions I had earlier in the evening. It frustrated me to no end. I really thought that my mind-reading ability would strengthen when I stopped drinking the tea, but it didn't seem to. Or the beer dulled all my senses, which was unfortunate in the current situation. Clarissa needs to teach me her tricks of blocking someone from reading their mind so I can find a loophole to reading every mind I desire.

It wasn't difficult to guess what Alaric was thinking. He loved being onstage, performing for his fans. And we were all fans. At the mere hint of a break, the crowd would chant, "More, more, more," and Alaric would turn around, shrug his shoulders to ask the silent question, and either Madigan would reply with a drum solo or Declan with a bass line, then he'd run his hand along my hair and tilt his head as if asking for my permission to continue. And what could I do? The crowd wanted him as much as I did. Maybe more. Who was I to deny them?

The more I drink, the fuzzier my brain gets. Weird how that works. Scott's still dancing with Maria, somehow remaining upright, though the forces of alcohol consumption should suggest otherwise. He grows brave with liquid courage and ducks his head to kiss her. Before his lips find their mark, however, some oversized jerk punches him square in the face and he goes flying into a nearby table. He scrambles to his feet faster than humanly possible and leaps to Maria's defense, only to be intercepted by his attacker.

I jump off the stage, ready to kick ass. Nobody messes with my brother and gets away with it. Alaric lands next to me, and much faster. He tears the ape off Scott and grinds him into the dance floor.

"What is the meaning of this?" he hisses.

"He went to kiss me girl," the asshole grunts.

"Your girl?" Alaric repeats. "I doubt that very much."

"It's true, I tell ya," he yells.

"Is it?" Alaric asks Maria, who has distanced herself from the fight.

She glances at Scott, then the asshole, then Alaric. She nods her head slightly.

Scott steps over to her. "You have a boyfriend?"

I hone in on Maria. The two sides I read from earlier reveal themselves again, and this time they war with each other. One shouting, "Yes! Yes!" the other yelling, "Be quiet."

Her face contorts as she fights for control. Maria is more than what she seems, but I can't tell what. Finally, one side wins. "His name's Elijah, and he was my boyfriend."

"Is!" he stammers.

"Was. We broke up."

"Why, ya lyin'—"

Maria slams her hand down, signaling him to stop. He goes still as if he couldn't say another word if he tried. I wish I had that effect on people. Would come in handy, especially when Scott doesn't want to shut up.

"Elijah, come. I'll take you home," she says, gesturing for Alaric to remove his foot from Elijah's chest.

"Do I know you?" Alaric asks as he follows her order.

She takes in his muscular form. "I'm local. I know lots of people," she winks.

Scott swallows.

So much for his night of romance.

Alaric ignores her advance. "If he so much as enters this club again when we're performing, I'll have him out on the street faster than he can say, 'Help.'"

She bows and backs away with Elijah. "Bye, Scott. Thanks for some excitement."

Scott's shoulders slump. "Glad I could be of service."

Freaking Maria and her oversized chump ex-boyfriend/boyfriend ruined the perfect night of debauchery I had planned for Scott. He was supposed to forget all his troubles for the evening, and now look at him. He's a sad drunk instead of a wildly entertaining one. If it wasn't so late, I'd find him another girl to hook up with, but the club's already begun to clear out. It'll be last call and time to leave anyway. I should get him out of here so he can get his mind off her while he's still standing.

Alaric reaches for me. "You're leaving, aren't you."

As much as I'd like to lean in and let him make me forget even my own name, Scott's my main priority tonight. I owe him that much. "He needs me."

"What if I tell you I need you?"

"You can walk yourself home. Look at him. He's flying in for a landing."

We watch Scott stumble across the dance floor with his arms out to the sides like an airplane, weaving in and out of the remaining dancers who aren't so much dancing as they are sucking each other's faces off.

He pulls me to his chest. "Can I come with you?"

Holding onto soberness is never easy, but after being drunk in Alaric's presence, I need all my senses. I manage to shake my head. "No. Scott needs me. He's eyeing up the stage like he's ready to move in."

Indeed the airplane lands, and the pilot, a.k.a. Scott, is slowly making his way up the stairs to the stage.

Sadness exudes from Alaric. "Why is it that you're always leaving me?"

"Believe me, I don't want to, but I promised Scott a night of fun and brother-sister togetherness. I should make sure he gets home all right. He doesn't know the countryside like I do. He hasn't had all the late-night rendezvous that I've had."

"I already miss you," he whispers into my ear.

I shiver involuntarily. "Uh-huh," I manage, already regretting my decision to leave without him.

He trails kisses down my earlobe, across my chin, and down to my lips. "Until we meet again," he whispers, breaking away from me.

"Uh-huh."

"Safe travels."

I blink. "Right, travels. Thanks!"

Scott and I stumble across the countryside, making our way to Granda's cottage. I don't remember it being so far from the club.

"I wish I'd let Alaric drive me home," I mumble to my companion.

"But then I'd be alone, and I . . . ," he giggles, "I can't see a darn thing. I'd probably wind up in a ditch and left for dead."

"That's probably not a bad idea."

"That hurts, Gigi. That really hurts."

"Did I injure your wittle-bitty overinflated ego? Oh wait —Maria did that when her psycho boyfriend came and tried to break your face."

"I could have taken him. I need a good fight to distract myself."

"Was she worth it?"

His mind envisions her dancing with him, and the way her chest pressed against his.

"As a distraction? Absolutely. But next time remind me to ask if there's a boyfriend in the mix."

"Would that have stopped you?"

"It might have. I don't like when people betray each other."

"They're not married."

"No, but breakups are messy. Unattached is much simpler and more convenient."

When we wander past the fairy mound, I get an idea. An awesome, terrible idea.

"Do you wanna try something?"

He straightens. "I thought you weren't going to experiment anymore. Stick to all-natural fermented products."

"No, I don't mean take something. I mean try something. As in, do you want to take a trip?"

He sprawls himself across Alaric's boulder. "Is it far? Because I'm really tired."

If he knew some of the things Alaric and I did on that boulder, he probably wouldn't be making himself so comfortable. But what he doesn't know won't kill him. Not in this case anyway. "Yes and no."

He lies back and stares up at the night sky. "If I don't have to walk, I'm game."

"I'm not even sure if it will work, but if it does, I think you'll like who we visit. Actually, I know you will."

He sits up. "Well, go on then. What are you waiting for?"

I reach into my front pocket for the spiral rock I have a habit of carrying around all the time now. "Hand?"

He drops his into mine. "You're not going to lick your palms and slap me across the face to sober me up, are you?"

"I only did that once."

"Twice. You've done it at least twice."

"Well, it was deserved. You were drunk."

"I'm drunk now."

"Yes, but you're mostly coherent, and when you're mostly coherent, you're tolerable."

"Glad to hear it, because as it stands right now, I'd like to remain mostly coherent for the foreseeable future. It really takes the sting out of everything, you know?"

"Sadly, I do. Now walk with me."

He pulls back. "I thought we weren't walking. I'm tired."

"Oh, god. Are you really whining right now?"

He lifts his chin. "I'm not whining."

"You are, trust me."

I'm not walking. I'm not walking, he chants.

"I can't believe you're taking advantage of my mind-reading ability to get your point across."

"You'd do it."

He's got a point there.

"Fine, I'll try it without you first. But if it doesn't work, you'll need to be with me."

He lounges across the boulder. "If I have to."

I wind my way around the fairy mound three times in

one direction. Each time I pass the entrance, I wave to him. He lazily waves back, content to watch me do all the work. After completing my third circle, I begin circling three times in the opposite direction. As I pass by the halfway point of my final lap, a heavy mist falls around me. It's so thick I can't see my hands in front of my face, let alone my brother. Familiar panic tightens my throat. I can't lose him. Not like this. Not again.

"Scott," I shout. "Scott!"

I call out again and again, but my voice gets lost to the mist. He can't hear me any more than I can see him. What if he wanders into the Otherworld without me to guide him in and guide him back? If I lose him now, I'll lose him forever. I know it.

"What is it you desire, Gigi Brennan?" A voice, neither man nor woman, echoes through the mist.

"Who the . . . ?" I spin around, but no one's there. "Who are you? What are you?"

"I am the All, I am the Knowing, and I know that which you are searching for."

Do not trust the mist.

Instantly, my nerves stand on end. But that other part, that curious part, wants to know.

"And what might that be?"

"You long for your Lizzie."

To hear her name said aloud is a siren call, and I will not be denied.

Do not share that which you know.

"Anyone who knows me would know that."

"Ah, but do they have the answers you seek? They are simpler than you think."

Lulled in by the voice and the promise of Lizzie, I will follow it anywhere. "Go on."

"The memory of friendship draws her near, but no longer herself, her purpose will prove deadly."

"Deadly for her or for me?"

"That is to be decided."

"Can her path be altered?"

"Two halves of a whole. The moon will awaken a hunger."

"So, she is a werewolf."

Werewolves I can deal with. The nightlock grows every night. The first batch should be ready for harvest soon.

"More than what you think."

The haunting promise of the words stabs me in the heart. "What else can she be?"

But before I receive an answer, the mist vanishes as quickly as it formed. I smack myself across the face to see if I'm asleep. The sharp sting against my cheek confirms I'm awake.

Wide awake.

I crouch into a fighting position. Legs wide, knees bent, fists up and ready. That's when I notice the blood gushing out of my right hand. The very one I cut open the night of Samhain to provide Scott with my blood to draw him back into the world of the living.

Raw anger wafts toward me, further heightening my senses. I am not alone.

I make a fist and pull my hand into my chest to stop the bleeding. I let my mind dial in on the root of the intense emotion. Nothing but blurriness meets me. I close my eyes and try again, but the only emotion or thought I can recognize is the sharp, poignant anger that can only come from someone wronged.

"Alaric?" I call out, but he doesn't answer.

It has begun.

I don't have to ask to know that the storm from the

prophecy, the one Clarissa keeps talking about, is on its way. I fear that it'll be more catastrophic than the imprisonment of Clayone. With most of my family and friends dead, I shudder to think what that means for the world as we know it.

The entrance to the Otherworld beckons me. The lure to enter draws me closer and closer until I am just a few feet away from the entrance.

That is but the coward's way.

I swallow hard, the temptation to escape overwhelming.

You are not finished yet.

"What if I want to be?" I whisper aloud.

You must right what's been wronged.

What if I'm wrong?

Follow your heart. It will guide you well.

My heart spoiled the day I lost Lizzie.

Then right it.

Wetness seeps into my clothing as a rain begins to fall. I pull at my necklace, drawing courage from the crystal Clarissa gave me. I take a deep breath and let oxygen creep back into my body.

I'm not proud of much of what I've done through the years, but I've never regretted anything until the day I showed Lizzie the spell book. That spell book opened an evil darkness to her, a darkness she would never have been exposed to otherwise.

And that spell book is here in Ireland. Breas has it.

I don't know how to right my biggest wrong, but if it clears the way for Lizzie's soul to enter the light, I will do it. I will do anything for Lizzie.

I open my palm and watch the blood coagulate. Lizzie told me she was summoned. I didn't know what she meant at the time, but now I think I know who summoned her. Him and his sick desire to create his own personal harem. He will pay for his actions. I'll make sure of it.

"Gigi! Gigi!" Scott yells as he barrels over to me. He pats my head and arms to prove to himself that I'm real and he's not seeing things. When satisfied, he yanks me into his arms to hug me. "It's you. It's really you. Thank goodness. I was so worried."

The mist confounds and confuses.

"It's me." A lone tear falls down my cheek.

Lizzie is out there somewhere, and soon she will thirst for me.

And I am powerless to stop it.

SPELL SCHOOL, TAKE TWO

*Y*ou'd think that as a reincarnated goddess one might possess an internal alarm system warning her when an intruder was entering her personal sleeping space, but you would be wrong. I know this personally because Clarissa took it upon herself to enter Granda's cottage, proceed to my room, and pull me out of bed by my ear.

"What are you doing?" I whelp as she drags me into the kitchen.

Granda rubs his eyes as he stumbles out of his room. "What is that terrible racket?"

"Tea?" Clarissa asks as she fills the kettle.

"Tea? That's all you can say after waking me up and yanking me out of bed at this ungodly hour?"

"Considering you're awake now, I'd call it a 'godly hour.' Or better yet, since you're back to pretending you're not Brigit, maybe we should call it, a 'not-so-godly hour.'"

I turn to Granda. "Is she always this mean?"

"Yes, actually. You'd think being more than fifteen

hundred years old would slow someone down, but you'd be mistaken."

She hums while she preps four mugs.

I pull up my hoodie to prevent any extra light from hitting my eyeballs. Between the alcohol and the mist, I've got one hell of a hangover. "Are you going to wake Scott too?"

She hands me a mug. "I already did. He should be coming out . . . ," she closes her eyes, then opens them, "now."

Scott steps out of his room looking bright-eyed and bushy-tailed. I hate him right now.

"Why didn't you yank him out of bed by the ear?"

"Because, Gigi, he was already awake. He sensed I was coming before I opened the front door. Isn't that right, Scott?"

He sits in the chair next to me. "Yes, actually. Why is that, do you think?"

"I suspect the tea blend you've been drinking is no longer warding off your magic since you've awakened," she says, adding Irish breakfast tea to each of our mugs.

"You mean when I realized I was Oegden?"

Sure, I've suspected Scott was Oegden, and he certainly has demonstrated some godlike attributes, but we've never talked about it. He's never declared himself officially as Oegden, but it appears now he has embraced it.

"When did that happen?"

"Last night when we were at that hill and the mist surrounded us."

That mist warned me about Lizzie. It seemed vengeful and unsympathetic. Brigit told me it confounds and confuses, yet Scott seems perfectly clear. "What did it tell you?"

"That my true love awaits me, and that soon we will be united."

"And from that you think you're Oegden? Maybe the beer made you hallucinate. You were completely drunk."

His green eyes bore into mine. "I saw her form in the mist."

"I couldn't see anything in the mist. How did you know it was her?"

"She shifted from a girl to a swan."

"The mist reveals truth in its own way." Granda pats Scott on the head. The obedient grandson fulfilling his destiny.

Mine, however, is much more tragic.

Clarissa pulls out the orange juice. "And what did the mist share with you, dear Gigi?"

The memory floods my mind. Lizzie stands before me, but not my Lizzie. Not the daughter of Jehovah's Witnesses who remained my friend even when her parents forbade it. Not the best friend who defended my honor whenever it was threatened. Not the girl who fell in love with a boy. No, this Lizzie thirsts for blood and howls at the moon.

Clarissa's eyes meet mine. The glass pitcher slips from her hands, smashing to the floor and shattering into a thousand pieces. The noise echoes through the cottage, vibrating off of us, wrapping our emotions in tiny shards. Her eyes widen. "The second prophecy has begun."

Oh yeah, I forgot that part. It seemed the least of my worries.

Granda folds his hands in front of him, faking calm, but the cracks in his mind tell me otherwise. "Clarissa, are you certain?"

Scott rests his hand over mine. "What did you see?"

"That Lizzie wants to kill me."

Scott coughs as he swallows and takes a moment to regain himself. "She's alive?"

I clasp my hands together to keep heat from forming. "Well, I wouldn't say she's completely alive."

"I don't understand."

Clarissa falls into a trance-like state, seeing but not seeing.

> "Bound by blood, yet split by purpose—
> Dead but not gone.
> Hunger quenched only by death."

"What does that mean?" Scott looks from me to Clarissa, then back to me, but the prophecy isn't finished yet.

"She's a werewolf," I whisper, before Clarissa continues.

> "Contained but not restricted,
> Controlling that once dedicated to another.
> The Storm approaches.
> Enemies emerge through stealth of step,
> Led by one with two faces.
> Force alliance,
> Or expire from unstoppable force."

Scott slams his fist against the table. Anger and confusion roll off him and fill the air around us with danger and contempt. "I don't understand. Why is there magic? How do werewolves exist? How did Lizzie return from the dead? Nothing in this world makes sense."

"It makes sense if you allow yourself to believe in things outside what you believe to be true," Clarissa says.

Her response makes her the target. Scott doesn't normally

go after someone, but in his current frame of mind, he directs his frustration at her.

"Easy for you to say. You're over fifteen hundred years old. You tell people what to believe. You tell them what's true."

Granda rests his hand on Scott's shoulder. He's trying to calm him, but the edges of Granda's mind are splintering. He's worried about us, and not sure what to do with this new revealing information about Lizzie, and he's never seen such power before, and it's kinda freaking him out though he's trying to act calm. I can finally read him almost as easily as I can read Scott, but given the reason, I don't want to. I pull away from him, because this rush of conflict and emotion might push me right off the edge.

Granda needs to work through his own stuff, but I can help settle Scott. I close my eyes and focus my calming energy toward him.

He swats at the air. "I don't want some artificial emotion given to me, and I don't want my anger taken away. I want answers. I want to know how monsters exist." He slams his fist down into the oak table. A rumble of thunder explodes with it, and the two halves fall into each other. Raw energy builds within him. Suddenly, it blasts out from him with enough power to kill a mortal. I throw up a shield to protect Granda and Clarissa, then flick my wrist and a book soars through the air and hits Scott on the side of the head.

It doesn't knock him out, but it hits him hard enough to make him realize what he's done. He looks at the broken table, then at us, before collapsing back into his chair. Tears stream down his face.

"What did I do? What's wrong with me?" he moans.

I step over the fallen remains of the table and embrace him. "We'll get through this. I promise you. We will get through this."

"Children," Clarissa says softly, "we need to continue your lessons. Now that your powers are no longer masked, you must learn how to control them."

Scott wipes his face with his sleeve. "I guess regular school is out of the question?"

"Is there a reincarnated god charm school? Because Scott definitely needs that."

He laughs. The negative energy built up around him softens. "If anyone needs charm school, it's you."

"Plaid skirts and knee-highs? I'm in. Maybe Hermione needs a roommate. I can practice potion-making on you." I shove my finger into his side.

He shoves me away. "As long as I can practice Defense Against the Dark Arts with you."

"They do go on, don't they." Granda says to Clarissa.

"That they do. With their power, they shouldn't be together. Separate lessons in separate locations would be best."

Vines shoot up through the floor and wrap around their wrists. "No, I can't be separated from Scott."

Clarissa flicks her fingers, and the vines fall away. "We won't separate you, but we need someplace capable of containing your magic. There is, perhaps, only one powerful enough to withstand your combined power."

"Gallean," Granda says.

"Yes. His realm offers a higher level of safety than this one," Clarissa adds.

"Realm? What is he, a king or something?" Scott asks.

Granda folds his hands in his lap, still trying to feign calm, but he's bothered by something. Sad, I think. I really try not to read his mind since he worked so hard to keep me out, but I can see, with the possibility of us leaving him, he is sad. "Do you think he'll take on two? I don't think he's ever done that before."

"We won't know until he meets them. He'll need to be enticed."

Enticed? As in parading us around like circus animals? I don't like the sound of that. And I know we need special training because we're two overpowered teenagers who don't know our asses from our bums, but how long will we be in this other realm? I don't mind running away from my problems—hell, I've spent a lifetime doing it—but now there's Alaric. And Lizzie. And even though she wants to kill me, I like having her around. Besides, if I'm off gallivanting in another realm I can't help her.

"I've heard murmurings he's no longer taking on students." Granda doesn't want us to leave. He keeps searching for excuses why we can't go.

Clarissa looks at the broken oak table, the vines, then at us. "Oh, I believe he can be persuaded. It's not often that two gods reincarnate together and are in need of mentoring."

"I'm not Brigit. I'm Gigi." I stubbornly cling to my present, rather than fully acknowledging my past.

Pretend all you want, but Clarissa knows. She can read your mind.

Quiet much?

"Whatever you say, dear." Clarissa says.

Granda doesn't want to admit it, but he knows Clarissa is right. There are, however, provisions to be met. In magic and astrological predictions, timing really is everything. He hurries over to grab his coat. "I need to do some research on moon phases. With the recent Super-Blue-Blood-Moon-lunar-eclipse phenomenon on Samhain, there may not be enough moon energy to open the portal to Gallean's realm. Let me see what I can find." He hesitates at the door, looks at Scott and me, then the broken table and the vines. "Clarissa, will they be all right without me for a few hours?"

Clarissa winks at us. "Oh, they'll be fine. We're going to

begin magic *charm* school, as the children suggested, since magic school was clearly too basic."

Scott folds into himself, becoming half his size. I finally discover what chagrined looks like.

"Perhaps mending furniture and flooring could be part of their afternoon recovery?"

Clarissa beams at us as if we hadn't just destroyed Granda's house. "I believe that can be arranged."

Granda pauses at the door. With a plan for our immediate future falling into motion, his mind begins to resolidify, closing off to me again. I doubt he even realized it opened. "Scott, Gigi, we will get through this. Our coven supports you and will fight for you, as will I."

"Thank you, Granda," Scott says, "I'm sorry about your table."

He winks at him. "What's some splintered oak among friends?"

I lift one of the vines. The dense, thick spine would make a formidable bind to tie someone up. "Sorry about this. They just kinda popped up."

He points at the torrential rain outside. We were so swept up in what was happening inside, neither one of us noticed what was occurring in the world beyond the cottage. "At least they didn't come in from the ceiling or we'd be swimming to our beds this evening."

I worry about him. He's old. A cold at his age could kill him. "Do you really need to go right now?"

"I'm used to it." He sticks out his hand. "Perhaps not this intense, but no matter. I'll survive. That's what slickers are for."

I wish it would stop raining.

No sooner do I think the words than sunbeams break through the clouds and shine down on the doorway.

"Well, that's convenient timing. Be good in your lessons,

children, and I'll be back later," he says, acting as if my thoughts and actions didn't just impact the weather. And maybe they didn't. Maybe it was purely coincidence that it suddenly stopped raining and the sun came out right when I wished it would stop, but the timing was eerily exact. Gram once told me there were no coincidences. But the weather? One reincarnated goddess can't affect weather patterns.

Perhaps not, but two can.

So, let me get this straight. Emotion flooded our minds, so precipitation flooded the outdoors? And what about the vines poking out of Granda's floor? Could I have controlled that?

Clarissa touches my arm, "Yes, you could have."

Scott's head twists around, reminding me of an owl. "She read your mind?"

"Evidently so."

"What a dark and terrible place to be."

"You got that right. Although," I pick up half of the table, "you're one to judge."

He lifts the other half. "True story."

Clarissa holds both halves of the table. "All right, children, since magic school clearly did not take into account your "Other" natures, magic charm school begins now . . ."

CHARM 101

"Magic charm school lesson one: Don't break the family furniture," Clarissa tells us before repeating a mending spell. She chants in Gaelic, but Scott and I know what she's saying.

She calls to Anu, the Earth Mother who sowed the seed for harmony with Dagda, Father Sky, who cared and nurtured it through the years. A warm current flows through our hands as we hold the pieces of the table together and she chants. The air crackles around us, and the veins of wood begin to pulse. We watch in amazement as the two halves ebb and flow until they form solid planks of wood with no indication they had ever been ripped apart.

"You may let it go," she tells us once she's finished. When we release the table, it stands tall and true as it's done for a hundred years or more. I run my hand along the surface, searching for an imperfection and finding none. Not one seam or splinter. "Wow," I whisper in awe.

Scott flattens his palms against the table and presses firmly against it. "Whoa. The split is completely gone."

We stand side by side in front of Clarissa. We respected

her before. We idolize her now. "Will you teach us how to do that?"

"You will repair Amorin's floor, but neither one of you shall fall into a repair mentality. To fix or repair means something went wrong. The goal of our lessons will be to avoid causing damage in the first place."

I crack my neck as I stand in front of one of the holes in the floor. "Seems simple enough. Though I do like breaking things."

Scott positions himself in front of the other vine hole. "That's an understatement."

"I'm not the one who broke the table. That was all you."

"Just trying to catch up to you. You're like a witchy wrecking ball."

The air crackles around me.

"Gigi, relax. You can't let people get to you," Clarissa instructs us.

"Annoying brothers don't count as people."

"That hurts, sis."

"Mend," she tells us, as if we have the slightest clue what we're doing. Sure, we watched her do her little hocus-pocus trick and heard the words, but that doesn't mean we know what the heck we're doing on our own.

I stare at the large hole the vine made in the floor, and I think of another hole. A giant freaking hole that took my two best friends—turning them into freaking werewolves intent on killing me And even though Ryan lived a few weeks afterward and Lizzie is still out there somewhere, I lost them both that day. I lost them, and I will never get them back. What good is reincarnating as a goddess if you can't save the ones you love? What good is learning how to mend a hole in the floor when you've got a gaping hole in your heart?

A loud clap of thunder shakes the cottage.

"Focus, Gigi, focus."

Scott shifts his attention to me rather than his hole. Rain starts to fall on the roof.

"Scott, you must focus too. Gigi is okay. You're both fine, but you need to learn how to control your power together or we will need to separate you."

The threat of us getting torn apart again stabs through the hole and right into my heart. That can't happen. I can't let it.

"Focus, Gigi. Focus," she reminds me again. "Scott, she's fine. Focus on what you need to do. Remember the rhythm of the chant. Focus all your energy on that hole in the floor. That hole you can mend. You can protect each other by fixing things you can fix."

I close my eyes and imagine a solid floor. I imagine Lizzie and Ryan standing beside us. We're holding hands. Together we form a circle. An unbreakable bond.

"That's it, Gigi, that's it. Now, say the words."

I call to Anu and Dagda and ask them to repair the floor.

I focus on what the floor looked like before a vine grew through it.

Only you can fix what's broken.

The stupid voice in my head breaks my concentration.

Split by purpose. Bound by blood. Unquenchable thirst.

"That's it, Gigi. Well done, Scott."

Pride spreads out from him. I open my eyes. The hole in front of him is gone. The one in front of me shimmers and shifts.

"*Deisigh*," he says, and the floor solidifies before my eyes.

"You beat me."

He pats my back. "Guess you're not the only teacher's pet."

I tap the floor with my boot. The spot where the vines came through sounds exactly like the rest of the floor.

"Wow."

"You're welcome."

"How did you do that so easily?"

Scott doesn't overthink what he just did. He gets right to the root of his true nature. "I like to fix what's broken."

Tears spring into the corner of my eyes. "Do you think I'll ever be fixed?"

"It doesn't matter. I'll always be with you."

"She needs to learn how to do it on her own. You two help each other more than you should," Clarissa says.

Scott didn't know I made the fireball for him, but he suspects it now. He's not mad or upset though, because he just helped me. He's not aware that we could be separated because of someone, like a werewolf best friend or a supposed-to-be-dead psycho witch killing me.

"Rather than breaking what's already mended," Clarissa continues, "let's go outside. You both need to practice focusing your energy."

"And that's different than what we've been doing?" I ask.

"Rose warned me you would be a test of patience."

"You talked about me?"

"Quite often."

"Gram was never one for the phone."

"Gigi, by now you should know there are much simpler ways of communicating."

"Enlighten me."

"We did correspond with letters—especially when we exchanged spells."

"Letter writing . . . sounds slow. Nothing magical about that."

"We met during meditative trips to the Otherworld."

"Did you ever meet face to face?"

"Yes."

"You came back to Vernal Falls? Did we ever meet?"

"Many times."

"Were you there the night Gram died?"

"I was."

"Why didn't you ever stay with us?"

"I used a portal."

Scott's forehead crunches up. "A what?"

"Lesson two: Portals exist," she says.

"Portals, as in Thor will leap from Asgard to Earth and back again?"

I put my hands up. "Spoiler alert: It blew up."

Scott rolls his eyes. "She knows I mean jumping from one universe to the next."

Clarissa pulls some herbs out of her apron. "While I'm not exactly up to date with popular culture, I did get the gist of what you were asking."

He knocks into me. "See?"

"Portal travel is not relegated just to Norse mythology. While it is possible to jump, as you say, from one realm to the next, there are considerable rules and astrological alignments that must be in place for such a jump to occur, and depending on the timing, the jump could be permanent."

"You'd be stuck there?"

"It's possible, yes. That's why Amorin went to consult a few experts who study the moon, universe, and the calendar, but when I went to and from Vernal Falls, I used a portal only accessible to those from Brigit's bloodline. As such, I was able to visit whenever I wanted."

"Did Gram ever come here?"

"No. She couldn't leave the property or the spells protecting you would be lifted."

Poor Gram. Her entire life was dedicated to me. She couldn't live with her love, Granda. She lost both her daughters. She was stuck taking care of a spoiled little witchy girl until she was killed by Clayone.

Clarissa pulls out an athame, similar to Scott's dagger, but with a more decorative handle. "Do not feel sorry for her. She never cared for travel."

I refuse to be appeased. It's annoying when everyone tries to make me happy. What about everyone else's life? Don't they deserve happiness too? "But she could have come to visit Granda."

"They saw each other often and spoke regularly. Do not lament for either of them."

I think of Alaric. "Can other people use portals?"

"You mean, did Alaric use one to get to Vernal Falls?"

Scott stiffens. "He was in Vernal Falls? You told me you just met him."

Clarissa just stirred the Scott trouble pot, and now I've got to talk my way out of it without lying since Clarissa's like a human lie detector. "I met him officially in Ireland, but he might have been keeping an eye on me back home."

"It was him at Metropol in Pittsburgh, wasn't it. I knew it. That bastard slipped you something. I'm going to kick his ass."

As his temper rises, the air around him swirls, shaping into a tornado.

I wave my hands up and down, trying to stop the energy buildup. "Scott, calm down."

He sweeps his arms up toward me, as if to brush away my efforts to try and stop him. He wants to let the anger swell with him. "Why would he be watching you? Who did he work for? I'll kill him. I will freaking kill him."

Vines would work to bind his arms, but they won't stop his anger. He needs to calm down or something terrible is going to happen.

"We don't need to get into all this right now. Scott, it's nothing. Calm down. Please calm down," I whisper while moving my hands up and down in a slow rhythm. The wind begins to subside. Clarissa chants beside me, matching my movement.

"Settle down, Scott. Settle down," I repeat while we work to slow the wind movement until it's nothing more than a gentle breeze.

He collapses to the ground and folds himself into a fetal position. "What's happening to me?"

Clarissa kneels down beside him. "Your power is awakening, and you have no idea how to wield it. Your natural instinct is to protect Gigi. If you perceive a threat, even if it's in your mind, energy builds up around you. You just need to learn how to settle it."

He latches on to the opportunity to make things better. He pushes himself up and crosses his legs. "And portal jumping will help me do that?"

Clarissa gestures for me to sit next to them. "Well, not portal jumping, but someone who can help the both of you use your power in a controlled setting. Today, though, we need to work on grounding your power."

He sighs. "Well, I'm definitely grounded right now." He palms the grass and reaches into it. "Why isn't Gigi having such a hard time?"

"Because I'm not a goddess."

He throws a clump of grass at me. "Gigi, we all know you are. Quit playing at that."

But still I refuse to give in. "How else can you explain why you're going Hulk, and I'm as gentle as a lamb?"

"Gigi, we all saw the vines shoot through the floor, and I was at the ruins with you and Clayone."

It is time to acknowledge and embrace your true nature.

"That was an act."

His jaw tightens. "Please don't lie to me."

"It was an act. I lied to Clayone."

A burn creeps up my throat.

"Mostly."

He smiles to himself. "I knew it. But why am I a master of disaster, and you're the oracle with the golden compass?"

"Because I've spent my life screwing up. Now I can act slightly insane and still seem normal compared to you."

Clarissa rests her hand on my shoulder. "She also digs in the dirt—soil grounds her. The earth is Brigit's conduit. Oegden, however, does not typically ground with the earth, though it does seem to be helping you right now. Instead, he draws from the air . . . that's why mini tornadoes keep springing up around you. You're going to need to reach out and draw grounding energy to you."

"That sounds complicated."

"Try it," she says.

"I don't know how."

"Yes, you do."

"I don't. I have no idea."

"Gigi, tell Scott who raised Alaric," she says then sits on the ground with her hands folded in her lap. Looking calm and peaceful. Grandmotherly. But she is far from maternal. She's poking a sleeping bear who will attack without warning.

"Please don't make me."

"Tell him who his father is."

"You know?"

"I've always known."

The air around him begins to swirl. "Who raised Alaric, Gigi?"

"It doesn't matter."

Scott awakens. He knows I'm not telling him something very important. "Who is his father?"

"It doesn't matter."

"Clarissa seems to think it does. Who is it?"

"Scott, I really don't—"

"Who is it?" The air forms and twists around him. Building. Spiraling. Being.

"Control it, Scott. You have to control it," I murmur to him.

"He'll get it. Believe in him," Clarissa whispers to me.

"Who. Is. It?"

Another mini tornado begins to form.

"Scott, it doesn't matter. Clarissa, do something."

"Tell him. He must know."

Frustration fills me. She shouldn't have brought up Alaric or his upbringing or his parents in the first place. It was impulsive and dangerous. "What good will it do?"

She lifts her chin in defiance. She refuses to let me compel or persuade her otherwise. "Tell him."

His anger continues to grow and spiral, especially since I've refused to tell him anything. "Gigi, tell me!"

I take a calculated risk that maybe Clarissa knows what she's doing and, in the end, everything will work out. "Carman raised him."

But instead of slowing, the tornado grows. He won't be able to control it soon.

"Tell him who else."

I bite down my annoyance at Clarissa. She better have a freaking reason for doing this. "Calliope. Calliope raised him."

Tears stream down his face. The tornado drops over him so he's standing in the eye of it. "And who is his father?" he shouts through it. His voice almost gets lost in wind.

I close my eyes. I can't watch Scott destroy himself, me, and probably the world. I have no idea why Clarissa is making me tell him, but I can't risk it building more. "Clayone."

The rush of air seems to disappear. The whirling sound of a steam engine fades. The sun peeks out of its hiding place. I slowly open my eyes, not knowing what I might find but aware that I can't ignore it any longer. The tornado hovers above him, ready to destroy everything in its path given the word. We are in the eye of the storm, and Scott decides whether we live or die.

"Clayone, the Original Werewolf, is his father," he whispers.

"Yes."

"My mom helped raise him?"

"Yes."

"Gigi, is he a werewolf?"

There's no point in withholding the truth any longer. "I think so."

He thrusts his hands out, palms open, as if inviting in company. Everything becomes very still. The calm before the storm. My jaw clenches, anticipating what comes next, but then I hear a bird sing, then another, and another, and finally a fourth one. Each with their separate song syncing into a single one. One by one they circle above his head.

"He's done it," Clarissa says beside me. "He's done it."

We watch as he brings his hands together in prayer position and the birds continue to fly around him.

"How did you know that telling him about Alaric would ground him? I thought he was going to blow us up."

"It could have gone either way, but he will do anything to protect you. He had to ground, or he'd destroy you."

"Kind of a big gamble, don't you think?"

"Well, considering the news Amorin is bringing us, we needed a true test. Anything else would feel contrived, and authentic discovery wouldn't take place."

"How did you know about Alaric?"

"Just as I used him to push Scott, the universe always brings Alaric to you as a true test of love."

"Is he a werewolf every time?"

"I'm not entirely sure, but I believe so."

"Why does the universe choose to test me in such a way?"

She turns to me and holds both my hands. "The universe is testing you both."

"Why?"

"True love is always tested, especially when one was once bound to another."

"You mean me and Breas."

"I do."

"He's a reincarnated god too, isn't he."

She pulls in a long slow breath. "No. He. Is. A. God."

It's my turn to suck in a breath. I don't know the difference between reincarnated gods and true gods, but I'm guessing there's something of a power struggle or some other type of significant drama to challenge us. "Why is he here?"

"You already know the answer."

"For me."

"For you."

SHADOW WORK

*G*randa brought bad news. Since the Super-Blue-Blood-Moon-lunar-eclipse-Samhain phenomenon, portal traveling will not be returning to its regularly scheduled programming anytime until at least the Shadow Moon, which evidently is also a rather rare occurrence. And, whoever this master sorcerer, Gallean, is—I'm picturing a blue cone hat with silver stars and Mickey Mouse ears—if he agrees to train us, we would stay in this Shadow Realm until the next Shadow Moon or a major celestial shift—whatever the hell that means.

In the meantime, Scott and I will meet Gallean in a seomra de rúin to see if he's interested in taking the job. Our physical bodies will remain on this plane, while our spirit selves will travel to meet him. According to Granda, "seomra de rúin" means an Irish room of secrets. Granda and Clarissa will anchor the seomra de rúin and supply our energy while our spirit selves are there. It all sounds a little too magical-make-believe to me, but nevertheless, here we are lying on Clarissa's living room floor.

"Do you have any pepper to go with that salt?" Scott asks as she forms a circle around us with a giant bag of salt.

"I'll take some provolone and tomato on my sandwich," I add.

Granda smiles down on us.

"What's so funny?" Scott asks him.

"One of the positive effects of a seomra de rúin is that bystanders can't hear anything that goes on while you're in there. It's completely silent, and I haven't had silence for some time now."

Scott pouts. "I thought you found us charming and playful."

"Sometimes. Other times I find the incessant chatter draining and tiresome."

Clarissa makes her way around the circle. "Oh, don't mind him. He's just lived alone for far too long. He's been in need of company. And for the record, I'm not using salt to draw the circle. I'm using chalk. I felt, for this spell, chalk would work well, especially once sealed with sage."

Following Scott's Come-to-Birds moment outside of Granda's cottage, we relocated to Clarissa's. Her large living room is conducive to seomra de rúin spell work because evidently Granda's cottage is too corrupted with our energy signatures.

We helped her set up the four corners within the circle. In each cardinal point, we placed a magically linked symbol to help ground the seomra de rúin. For the North, a bowl of crystals to represent the Earth; in the East, a sage bundle to represent Air; in the South, candles to represent Fire; and in the West, a chalice with water to represent—well—Water. Scott and I will serve as the fifth element, Spirit. And the gods know we've got a lot of spirit between us. I'm just not sure if it's the type of spirit Clarissa and Granda had in mind.

Granda kneels down by our heads. "Children, remember,

your physical bodies will remain here. Your metaphysical beings will venture to the seomra de rúin. If Clarissa and I build it correctly, you will feel like you're in an actual place, though you've never been there before. Every object, every piece of furniture, every room, every plant, every book represents Gallean's place."

I clear my throat. This whole seomra de rúin venture has me out of sorts—as if the whole Breas-is-a-god-and-bound-to-you thing or the your-best-friend-wants-to-kill-you thing wouldn't achieve a similar result. "What if you didn't build it correctly? What would happen then?"

Scott tsks. "Of course Gigi has to be the naysayer of this expedition."

"Just wondering."

"It is, in fact, an important question," Clarissa says as she finishes completing the circle. "If one aspect of the space is incorrect, the seomra will collapse into itself."

Scott swallows. "And what will happen to us?"

"Not to worry, dear. It sounds much more dramatic than what actually occurs. You'll awaken from your slumber."

Scott rubs his hands together. He can't wait to go to this other realm. He's got a major Marvel superhero complex. "Okay, seems straightforward. When do we get started?"

Granda chuckles. "It takes a tremendous amount of magic to create a seomra de rúin. As such, we need to make your visit worth it."

The seomra de rúin will drain Clarissa and Granda for days. They didn't tell us that part, but I can tell. I don't want them to expend themselves and put themselves at risk from us (if one of us has a magical episode before we get properly trained) or from a rogue werewolf BFF who wants to kill me. They refuse to listen to reason and brush off my concerns as if I don't know what I'm talking about. But I keep trying to find a way out of seomra de rúin. "Will he be expecting us, or are we just dropping in?"

Clarissa lifts her athame and lays it across her sage bundle, then traces the bundle with the blade before placing it back down. "Don't worry about us, Gigi. If he pays attention to the signs, which he always does, he'll know you're coming. Your trip will be successful."

"Do we tell him who we are?" Tension builds around Scott as he worries about the damage he already caused. I lay a calming shield around him to lull him. His power pokes at the sides, testing for weakness.

Granda raises his cup, which resembles my missing Chalice of Healing but is nowhere near as ancient. He places his bundle of sage in it. "When he sees you, he will know."

Scott wants to rid himself of his power, and the sooner the better. He's anxious to begin training. "Do we ask him if he'll teach us?"

Clarissa lights her sage bundle and tips it toward Granda. He uses hers to light his then takes it out of his cup. Thin wisps of smoke begin to spiral in the air above them. "He will."

"How can you be so sure?"

"Though he may be the greatest wizard of all the realms, the opportunity to instruct two reincarnated gods, whom he worships as fervently as we do, will not allow him to refuse such an honor."

It makes me uncomfortable when Clarissa and Granda act like we are something more than our Earthly forms. I much prefer it when they're ordering us around and telling us not to bicker.

Granda waves his sage around the outside of the circle. "One more thing. Though you'll only be there with your metaphysical beings, you can be hurt and feel pain. You can feel hunger, sadness, even joy and love."

"I've had enough love complications to last me an eternity," I mumble to myself, trying not to think about my alleged true love, Alaric, and all the tests we are repeatedly put through, or of Breas and what our once-bound relationship means today, and obviously failing at both miserably.

Clarissa lifts her arms in the air, preparing to channel the power needed for the seomra de rúin. "Your life challenges will remain here, but you will feel other emotions there. Keep each other close, and don't mind Gallean. He bears no resemblance to anyone you've encountered yet. Let's begin . . . Scott, Gigi, lie flat please."

The smoking sage settles down on us, and they chant familiar spell words calling on the elements and their cardinal points.

"Close your eyes," Granda whispers. "Answers will find you."

I wake up with a jolt. The brilliant blue sky above me lets me know I'm no longer in Clarissa's house.

I shove the body next to me. He certainly feels real to me. "Scott, wake up. Scott."

He jerks awake and leaps into a fighting stance—legs wide, his silver dagger out of his leg strap and into his hand faster than humanly possible. But I guess reincarnated gods aren't exactly human. "Where are we?"

I look around. Four walls surround us, but we're not closed in. We landed on what appears to be a laid stone terrace. Four giant oak trees at the four cardinal points anchor a deck on the second floor. "I don't know. A courtyard, I think. Look at the ironwork on the railings."

"You're admiring architectural details rather than worrying about where we are?"

"I mean, yeah. Look at this place. It reminds me of a keep for a knight."

A deep growl echoes through the courtyard.

"Or a powerful wizard. Stay behind me," he whispers.

"What are you worried about? These are only our metaphysical bodies, not our real ones."

"Grrrrrrrrrrr."

He slides in front of me. "Do you remember what Granda said?"

"Grrrrrrrrrrr."

The source shifts to our side. With Scott no longer guarding me, I edge toward it. "More or less. I didn't really pay attention. That's what you're for."

He moves in front of me. "He said that we can still feel things. Hunger, sadness . . . and pain."

"Grrrrrrrrrrr."

Now the sound comes from behind us. Behind me. The hairs on the back of my neck stand up, and I crouch into a combative stance. I hold my palms a few inches apart and try to conjure some heat, but I've got no magic here. No spark.

"He also said love. Maybe that's your future girlfriend growling."

Suddenly, a giant bear leaps from an open archway and barrels down at us. Teeth bared. Mouth foaming.

It rears on its hind legs in front of me, stretching its mighty claws out at me. Scott lunges between us, his dagger transforming into a giant silver sword. He swings it like a baseball bat, aiming for the beast's gut.

Before he can discover what it ate for breakfast, the bear drops down on its front legs inches from the edge of the blade. It swings its head from the weapon to us and back to the weapon as if debating whether charging us is worth the risk.

Scott takes an aggressive step forward in challenge. The

bear falls back, releasing a warning roar louder than thunder. Energy crackles around us. I wince, knowing what's coming next and unable to prevent it or shield Scott from the magic.

Scott, however, is unfazed by the angry beast. He pulls back his sword and swings. The weapon becomes an extension of him. Before it finds its mark, the bear darts away. When it's safely out of Scott's reach, it paws the ground. Its claws rip across the stone floor, sending shivers down my spine. A strange chuffing sound rumbles from its chest. Dark eyes rimmed with a golden brightness watch us.

Energy crackles in the air, waiting for a power to direct it. I try calling to it, but it refuses to answer. A lightning strike hits the bear, filling it with power. The beast charges at us like a tractor trailer on rocket fuel. The bear's teeth clamp down on Scott's forearm, and it dashes away before he can slash at it.

Scott releases his own roar as he raises his sword. Blood drops from his arm, staining the stone red. "You coward. Fight me!"

I reach up and try to pull his wounded arm to me. "Scott, you're hurt."

"It's nothing," he says through clenched teeth. "Get behind me. I need to finish this."

The bear watches us battle with each other. Me, trying to examine the wound. Scott, refusing to cooperate.

"Fight me!" Scott growls, stepping toward the bear. The bear stomps at the stone terrace. It chuffs in warning at Scott, but Scott continues to advance. Instead of rising to Scott's challenge, the bear slowly backs away until it disappears under one of the wings of the terrace.

More energy crackles in the air. I try again to conjure something, anything, but there's not an ounce of energy in this place that I can draw from.

A figure appears from the same passageway the bear

escaped down. As it steps into the light, we can see it's a large, hairy, muscular man wearing a leather tunic and a long flowing cape.

"Who sent you?" His voice is rough and gravelly, as if his vocal cords haven't been used for a very long time.

Scott raises his sword. He doesn't trust the giant of a man any more than I do. His wild brown hair doesn't fit the wise white-haired wizard image we have in our minds. Thanks Rowling and Tolkien. "Who are you?" Scott counters.

The man eyes the sword, then us. "I asked you a question first, Angry One."

The tone of his voice assures me he won't hurt us. I try to step in front of Scott, wanting to get closer, to speak with the stranger, but Scott refuses to let me pass. I try to strong-arm past him, but it's no use. The big oaf blocks my every step. Instead of creating more of a scene than we've already done, I remain hidden by Scott's body, which has grown about fifty times larger than I remember.

"Amorin and Clarissa sent us."

"What are you doing?" Scott hisses out of the side of his mouth.

The stranger considers us, then the sword, then us again before deciding that either we're telling the truth or we aren't a threat. To demonstrate his belief that we won't harm him or him us, he sits down in one of the chairs in the middle of the courtyard and gives us a wide smile. "I saw you coming, Bold One, along with your brother, the Angry One."

I creep out from behind Scott. "Are you Gallean?"

He studies me. His deep brown eyes are rimmed with gold. "What do your instincts tell you?"

"You're Gallean, and you were the bear."

"Correct on both accounts. Now sit, and bring the Angry One with you."

I walk over to Gallean, but his nickname usage needs to

be addressed. "I find it insulting you consider him the Angry One. Scott's nothing but light and goodness."

Scott folds his arms across his chest, his sword dangling beside him looking the very opposite of light and goodness. "I can defend my own honor, thank you very much."

I worry about that wound on his arm. It's already clotted, but magic animal bites probably cause more harm than real ones do. "We need to clean that bite before it becomes infected."

Scott rolls his eyes. I'm not doing anything to help his tough-guy image. He doesn't want to look weak in front of Gallean. "It's not real, remember?"

"Your scream sounded awfully real when he bit you." I reach for his arm, and he pulls it away. It's my turn to roll my eyes at him before glaring at Gallean. "Real nice, by the way. Why'd you have to bite him?"

Scott worries that I'm being so straightforward with our former attacker, but I'm not the Bold One for nothing.

Gallean folds his hands in his lap, appearing positively dainty compared to the ferocious beast from moments ago. "I wanted to see just how brave he was. I've always heard about Oegden's dedication to his sister. I wanted to see it in action for myself."

Scott is unfazed by Gallean's pronouncement of his obsessive compulsion to watch out for me, but of course, I've got something to say about it.

"A little sick, don't you think?"

"Injuries are only temporary here, but I haven't seen Moralltach for centuries. How is it that you came in possession of it?"

"Moralltach?"

"Your sword, Moralltach, the Great Fury."

Scott admires the blade. "It was a dagger I keep tied to my leg. It changed into a sword when you attacked us."

"Forgive my other nature. He is a deterrent to trespassers."

I fold my legs up to make myself comfortable before taking in the stone building surrounding the courtyard. There are three more archways matching the one the bear emerged from and disappeared into. "Do you get many here?"

"Infinite numbers have arrived in this seomra de rúin. Most times the seomra folds in on itself and I don't actually need to appear. Occasionally some get past the initial landing. None have gotten as far as you. That's how I came to suspect that you are more than what you seem. Few from your realm have come for a visit. As to whether I get many trespassers, the answer is yes. They are considerable."

"Do you greet all your guests in such a friendly manner?" Scott runs his hand along the blade, admiring its shine and its sharpness.

"Most are not as lucky as you."

"Do people know you're a bear shapeshifter?" And, yes, I do possess an almost-stalkerish interest in shapeshifters and their process.

"Actually, I can shapeshift into any animal. I chose the bear for its size and its initial impression. It's typically enough to deter unwanted company." Gallean's eyes return to Scott's sword. "Now, Moralltach spilled much blood during the battles of the Tuatha Dé Danann and the Fomorians. As I mentioned, its nickname is the Great Fury, and that title is well deserved."

As Gallean talks to Scott about the sword and the different battles it played a winning role in, I study him. The sharpness of his cheekbones and jawline starkly contrast his inviting brown eyes. There's warmth in them I wouldn't expect from such a strong man as evidenced by his bare, muscled arms. He looks nothing like what I assumed the most powerful wizard of all the realms would look like.

He turns to me. "You expected someone fragile, didn't you."

My cheeks burn with embarrassment. "You can read my mind too."

"That, and the lines of your forehead suggest as much."

"How old are you?"

"Age matters not."

"How many years did it take you to master magic?"

"One does not master magic. One learns to use it to his or her advantage."

"And how does one go about doing that?"

"Ah, the root of your arrival. You believe the Angry One needs more time than you."

There he goes again, mocking my brother. "I really find that nickname offensive."

"You think you are the only one capable of anger?"

Suspicion laces Scott's eyes.

"No, I didn't say that."

"But you think it. And you are correct. The Angry One will spend more time in this realm than you, but not for reasons that you think."

Scott leans forward. "For what then?"

Gallean snaps his fingers. "That is for you to discover once you physically arrive."

"So, you will train us?" Even I can hear the resignation in my voice. I feel conflicted about Gallean agreeing to train us in the Shadow Realm for a number of reasons, mainly involving leaving Alaric and Lizzie behind, but also because Gallean just confirmed that Scott and I will eventually be separated, and I just got him back.

"I will guide you for a length of your journey."

Relief at the thought of a brief escape from Breas and

Kensey, and the threat that facing Lizzie brings, and even the truth of Alaric's true nature overcomes my reluctance. "When do we begin?"

"Anxious to escape your difficulties?"

Yes, I am anxious to escape all those things, but I will not let him lead me down that path of complications. "How do we leave the seomra de rúin?"

"You each need to find a key within my keep to release yourself."

I stand up to take in the expansive courtyard and living quarters. "It'll take hours."

"It could take weeks. You'd best get hunting. Unless, of course, you choose to stay here to avoid what awaits you at home."

I pull back my shoulders and stick out my chin. "I don't run away from my problems."

Hot flames lick at my throat. I gasp, grasping my neck.

Scott rushes over. "Gigi, what's wrong?"

I brush him off. "It's nothing. Let's get out of here."

"On the night of the Shadow Moon, I'll be waiting."

Scott glances at Moralltach, then at Gallean. "No grizzly encounters next time, right?"

Gallean throws his head back and laughs. "I make no promises, but I will try to restrain myself."

Scott glances at the table beside him and picks up a key. "That was easy."

"You may leave now, or you may wait for your sister."

Scott settles into the chair next to this man, this great wizard, who he now finds charming and entertaining, especially after his bearish greeting. "She could be a while. You should see her room."

I'm annoyed that Scott once again fits in and makes friends wherever he goes, even when we're in another dimension, while I'm the odd one out, forced to find some stupid key so I can get out of here. "You two can leave. I'd hate to make anyone wait on my account."

Gallean rests his feet on the table. "Don't worry. I'm in no rush."

Scott mimics him. "Neither am I."

I roll my eyes and stomp up the stairs in search of a key to release me from this hellish realm.

GET REAL

*T*here were three things I wanted to do when I woke up from the seomra de rúin. First, I wanted to punch Scott in the face because he went along with being labeled the Angry One—even though that title clearly belongs to me—and because he became BFFs with a bear-wizard who attacks his visitors.

Second, I wanted to find Breas, string him up by his ankles for bringing Lizzie back from the dead and turning her into a psycho werewolf who wants to kill me, beat him until he finally breaks down and tells me where he's keeping her, and then end his miserable life on Earth along with that in every other realm he's ever existed.

For the record, I don't actually know if I can cause him real or magical pain because of my Brigit-the-Goddess-green-magic limitations and peace-loving nature (funny, I know), but I figure that a legitimate threat of violence and the promise of lifelong torture might encourage him to help me locate her.

Third, I wanted to find Lizzie, and when I do, I need to figure out how to prevent her from wanting to rip my throat out. And when that feat is achieved—and I have the utmost faith in my ability to figure out that puzzle—I need to see if we can extract her werewolf nature. Then all the world would rejoice because my dear Lizzie would be alive and well and nonmagical.

I swung at Scott as soon as we "landed," but he must have sensed my wrath and rolled away from me. It's annoying how freakishly fast he's become since he's embraced his inner god.

"Nice try, but you'll have to start working out if you want any chance to win against me."

"Don't worry. I'll find you and get you when you're unsuspecting and ignorant of my presence."

"Oh, joy," Granda says, clapping his hands together. "The two of you made it through to the other side and returned with your gregarious nature intact."

He tries to sound as if he's upset that we began talking the moment we woke up, but I can tell he's overjoyed that we managed to visit Gallean. I can't read his mind completely, but since the "explosive god" episode when his blocking measures cracked, I find it easier to get a sense of his emotions.

"So, it was a success then?" Clarissa asks as she smudges the chalk out of one section of the floor so we can pass through.

Scott leaves the circle first. "It was. Thanks for letting us know that Gallean is a shapeshifter who prefers to meet his guests as an enraged grizzly."

I run my fingers through my hair and throw it up in a ponytail as I follow him. "Clarissa did tell us that he *bears* no resemblance to anyone we've ever met before."

Scott smacks his head. "Now I get it, but still not funny."

"It was a little funny," Clarissa grins as she leads us over to the benches. "Now drink this," she says, handing each of us a glass.

I smell mine. Some herbs I recognize. Others I don't. "Shouldn't we stop drinking Gram's tea, so we can draw from our witchiness."

"You mean bitchiness, right?" Scott says, sniffing his.

I give him the middle finger. Godly or not godly, some things will never change.

Clarissa sets the pitcher down without pouring herself or Granda any. "What you decide to do with Rose's magic-suppressing tea is your own decision. In actuality it might help curb some of the power surging through you. But this is my own blend. Made for recovery and strength."

Granda waves at the air. "Enough of this small talk, what did he say?" He leans forward. "Did he agree to train you?"

We glance at each other. Sadness shifts between us now that we know we won't be together in the Shadow Realm for the same length of time. Gallean didn't explain why or what will happen, just that Scott would be there longer than me.

I know I will die. That's what the next prophecy means. It means Brigit will die. But if that means Scott will live, I'm okay with that.

Clarissa rests her hands on mine. "It doesn't, and you won't. I admit that I can't see everything, but that's not the reason why you and Scott will be separated."

Clarissa's back to her mind-reading tricks, I see.

"Then what is it?"

Time will explain everything, Brigit answers for her.

"You see?" she smiles. "Now, drink your tea. You need fortification."

"Still didn't answer my question . . ." Granda says.

"He'll train us," Scott replies.

Granda leans back in his chair. All the energy and excitement quickly depart him. "That's wonderful news."

He needs to drink some of Clarissa's tea too, then take a nap, but I've got a ton of questions for Brigit's most dedicated follower. I drain my mug and set it on the table beside me. "Clarissa, I'd really like to speak with you."

She pats me on the hand. "I know you would, but I am not up to long explanations and stories tonight. Perhaps tomorrow?"

Clarissa and Amorin look like they're going to pass out. I pick up the pottery pitcher. "We're not the only ones who need fortification."

"That's not for mortals to drink."

I chant while I wave my hands over the top of the liquid. When finished, I pour them each a glass and offer it to them.

"Now it is."

The tea helped them, but they both needed to rest for the remainder of the evening. Scott promised to come back and check on Clarissa later, and we took Granda home.

With Clarissa unable to answer even one of my gazillion questions, I turned to Dad's journal. Though the pages with his careful handwriting soothed me, I didn't discover anything new.

Sometime around eight, I informed Scott that I needed to go to the Cathedral. He questioned my true intentions, assuming I was sneaking over to Alaric's. I suppose that was deserved and warranted. In all the time we lived in Vernal Falls, never once did I ask to go to the library on my own. But Mr. Smarty Pants hasn't been to the Cathedral yet. He doesn't realize the number of books it houses or the age of them or even that there are dark magic ones—at least when Carman was working.

My purpose in going was twofold. First, I needed to find out why I disliked Breas from the moment we first met. I won't deny there was—okay, still is—chemistry between us, but the voice within me, and I'm not sure if it's Brigit talking or another voice trying to sneak out, doesn't like him.

And second, when I get that information, I can use it as leverage to find out where he's hidden Lizzie. Then I can rid the world of him. I guess that's three reasons. I never was strong in math.

Scott gave me a flashlight and his dagger before I left. After we finally returned to this plane—my god it took me *forever* to find the key—Moralltach shrank back into dagger size, no longer bearing the mark of a god—which makes bringing it along much more convenient, because I'm no expert but my guess is that a giant sword is bound to raise suspicion. I'm just spitballing here but, given the right circumstances, I suspect he could call Moralltach to come to my defense. I tried to refuse him because I didn't want him unarmed when he went to check on Clarissa later, but he laughed at me. Actually laughed, informing me that he was plenty strong without the dagger. After witnessing his table-splitting this morning, I suppose that's true.

On my way to the Cathedral, I thought about my first night in Ireland. When Dad and I landed, I couldn't wait to explore the grounds of the Cathedral and search the building for answers to my questions. I thought the answers would spew from a fountain of knowledge, but alas, I haven't found that salmon yet. Since then I've discovered that no answer is straightforward. They're laced in metaphor and allegory, and they can drive a sane person freaking bananas, so imagine how I'm feeling right about now.

I use the side entrance where I first met Carman. I hate admitting it, but it creeps me out. I keep thinking she'll pop out at any second. It makes me mad that I was so trusting of her and so gullible, because I've never been trusting or gullible. I suspect I was spelled.

Praise the gods or my natural human repellant factor that no one comes out to meet me this time. There's no time to make nice with some stranger when I could be searching for answers to my many questions.

I wander through the rows of books, pulling out the ones that speak to me either because of the title or age of the book, or because Brigit tells me to. More than once I stop and look around. I have the strangest feeling that someone is watching me. I brandish the dagger so if I am in fact being watched, he or she will realize that I'm armed and ready to slice. Scott's dagger looks small, but I know it is a mighty sword. Moralltach, the Great Fury, as Gallean called it.

I search the shelves for the werewolf book that Carman gave me, but it's not in the library. Not that I can find anyway. I pinch my pointer fingers to my thumbs with my palms open to allow energy in and murmur a search spell. I try a few times in different ways, but get nothing. She probably took it with her. I imagine a how-to werewolf manual would be very valuable in the right circles. I grab other books that catch my eye. Books that might have magic or include Celtic folklore or Celtic mythology, because actually they're not the same thing, along with some Catholic ones on Brigit.

I set the towering pile of books down on the table and begin leafing through the top one, searching for something, anything, that will give me answers for who Breas is to me and, with any luck, what I can do to stop him.

The subsection "Brigit: The Healer" gives me pause. I've done everything in my power aside from shoving my fingers in my ears and singing "La la la-la la" to avoid learning or reading anything about the Goddess, but now, confronted with my true identity in black and white, it's hard not to.

"Brigit of Kildare, the patron saint of the Cathedral, is believed to be based on the Celtic Goddess Brigit. The church championed her as a woman of faith who sacrificed for the greater good. She was known for her generosity amongst the poor. She often gave food stores away to the needy, rather than ensuring the nuns would have enough sustenance to last the winter. When questioned on this subject, she often replied, 'We will be provided for.'"

Her selflessness doesn't sound like me in the least.

You would die to protect the ones you love.

You are fiercely protective of your people.

You risk your life every day just by reincarnating.

"And thanks for the cheerleading pep session," I murmur.

A cool breeze flicks the page. I take it as a sign to turn it, and I find "Breas" and "husband" at the bottom of it. Seeing the two words in print makes the whole thing way too real. And though any recount of the Goddess or Saint Brigit is an interpretation by the author, some of it must be based on truth.

"But still, married to him? I mean what a fucking asshole."

"Are you talking to someone?"

I jump up, dagger in hand, ready to swipe at whoever dared sneak up on me. And when I realize who it is, it's even more surprising. "Maria?"

"Sorry to startle you, Gigi. You were so intent on whatever you were reading that I didn't think you knew I was here, but then you said something aloud and I thought you were talking to me."

I drop the dagger on the table. "Clearly I didn't. What are you doing here anyway? Don't you have a jealous boyfriend to calm down?"

She drags her finger along the spines of my book stack. I think about breaking her finger for molesting my books, but they really aren't my books. Technically they belong to the library. Still, I found them.

"I suppose I deserve that. Elijah doesn't know how to let

go of love lost. To be honest, I think he's obsessed with me, though I really don't know why. I mean look at me," she says, gesturing to her more-than-ample boobs and nicely formed hips. She's got more in the body department than I do, that's for sure.

"It must be terrible searching for shirts revealing just the right amount of cleavage. And raven black hair—what a drag. I've got half a head of it and can't do anything with it."

"Gigi, your hair marks you as unique. White with black underneath? I love it, but you made your point. I shouldn't complain about the body I've been given."

"Strange phrasing, but whatever. Now, if you don't mind, I've got work to do."

She lifts a book off my stack. She's really asking to get her ass kicked. *"Moon Phases and Astrological Signs.* Are you into astrology or metaphysical studies?"

I tug the book away from her. "Neither. I was under the impression that you were leaving."

She plops herself into the chair opposite me. "If it's not too much bother, I'll just sit here and read. The Cathedral clears my head when I'm confused, and after meeting Scott, I'm very confused."

My palms flicker with heat. I clamp them together. "Listen, I don't like most people—and that's nothing personal against you, it's just a fact. Plus, I'm not a big conversationalist. And whatever occurred between you and my brother is none of my business. I can assure you that he will be more than fine without you."

She winces. "Ouch. You certainly are direct."

"I certainly am."

"Just how I like her," Alaric whispers in my ear.

I initially stiffen. He took me by surprise. But then I relax into his still-bent-over chest. "Where did you come from?"

"Conjured from thin air," he teases, knowing I'd catch his

hidden joke. "Actually, I came to rescue you from the clutches of intellectual pursuit."

Maria jumps up from her chair, drops her head, and edges away from us. "I didn't mean to impose. I'll be going," she says and disappears behind the nearest row.

I lay the book I took from her on the table. "That was weird."

"What was? That you didn't laugh at my joke or that she left without saying goodbye?"

He's playful tonight. He makes me want to be playful too. "Well, I've got a lot to work with, but let's go with the most glaring. About two seconds before you showed up, she made herself comfortable and planned to tuck in for the night, even though I told her in no uncertain terms that she needed to leave."

"Do I need to leave?" he whispers as he nuzzles my neck.

"You are a much-needed diversion after my day."

He breathes into my neck. "I thought you'd show up at my house last night after you dropped off Scott. I know you know the way."

I reach to close the section about Breas being my husband, or at least the Goddess Brigit's husband at one time, but a heavier breeze takes the pages and shuffles them like cards in a deck.

"Did you see that?"

"What? The way you twitch every time I do this," he says, trailing his hand down my side to the exposed skin between my shirt and my jeans.

I want to soak in the way my body tingles whenever he touches me, but strange things are afoot at the Cathedral.

"No, did you feel that breeze that keeps turning the pages of my book?"

I stand to investigate, but he embraces me from behind. "No, I've been preoccupied with you."

A cold breeze hits us both as he bends down to kiss me. He blinks, stunned.

"You felt that, didn't you? Come on, let's go check it out."

I reach for his hand.

"Gigi, I will follow you anywhere."

"That's what I was hoping you'd say."

TROUBLED TUNNELS

*a*laric takes hold of the back of my shirt in the same fashion Scott did last night at Hell's Gate, and we search for the source of the mysterious breeze. We wind our way through the rows, exploring every nook and cranny, finding nothing but dead ends.

"Do you see anything?" I whisper, tracing my hand along the shelves, hoping a door will pop open and announce, "This way."

He pulls me to a stop. "Hold on." He closes his eyes and inhales deeply.

I figure the faster we get the awkwardness of him being a werewolf out of the way, the faster we can resolve the great mystery of our past lives together and our current relationship. "Are you working your wolfie sense?"

He pulls his lips to the side, looking kind of adorable. "Yes, but give me a second."

"One."

He wraps his hand around my mouth.

Normally when someone attempts such a maneuver, they wind up with inoperable nuts for at least a week, but I know he's doing it for my own good because sometimes I just can't keep my mouth shut.

He breathes in again and stands still.

I lean into him. The surprised closeness derails him and he loosens his grip over my mouth.

"Anything?"

He reaches for my hand. "Follow me."

It's my turn to pull back. "I like to lead."

We stand toe to toe, but not head to head. He towers over my miniaturized frame. "You know I'm a werewolf, right?"

Nothing to see here folks. This conversation is totally normal. Totally mundane. "Yeah, so?"

He edges closer, so now some of his boy parts are touching some of my girl parts. "Do you know what position I am in my pack?"

I sense where he's going, and I'll play his game. "No. And since I'm not part of your pack, it doesn't matter."

He grins, leaning closer. "Oh, really? You want to argue with the alpha?"

I reach up and yank his head so his lips dangle above mine. "I told you, I'm not afraid of you."

"You keep telling me that, but you should be." Without warning, he throws me over his shoulder and carries me down a side aisle.

I swing my arms and legs, trying to break free. "Put me down. Where are you taking me?"

He slides me off his shoulder and back on my feet. "I thought you wanted to solve the case of the mysterious breeze."

"And you've cracked the code, Sherlock?"

He stands in front of a long tapestry of Brigit. She's holding a candle in one hand and a plant in the other, walking in a garden with a fountain in the background. I try not to linger on the image long. I don't need to get into a personal identity crisis right now.

"Well, have you?" I prompt him.

He pushes the tapestry aside and presses against a seemingly solid stone wall. "It's elementary, my dear Watson: a trap door to what appears to be a secret passage."

The wall gives way and recesses into a tunnel.

I tap him on the chest as I pass by and step into the darkness. "Bravo, bravo."

He pulls my hand, stopping me.

"What now?" I sigh. Who has time to flirt when there's a new adventure close at hand?

"I lead."

"Alpha male much? No, it might not be safe for you."

He brushes past me, "And that's why I'm going first. Plus, I can see really well in the dark. Now, grab on."

"Another wolf thing?"

He flashes green glowing eyes at me. "You can say that."

"Oh . . ." is all I manage as I hand him Scott's flashlight. I bunch his shirt in my hands, and together we plunge into the darkness.

When we've gone twenty paces, he whispers, "Are you scared yet?"

"No," I protest, although the tunnel is pretty foreboding. Narrow stone walls, pitch black—basically every stereotypical tunnel you've ever seen in a horror movie.

"Give it time."

My palms twitch with heat. "I think I can handle myself."

"We'll see about that."

Scott's flashlight worked for a few hundred feet, but then the lightbulb began to fade.

"I'm guessing you didn't bring spare batteries," he whispers.

"You guessed correctly. I thought you could see in the dark."

He turns to me, his green wolf eyes glowing. "I can, but you can't."

I rub my palms together and decide it's now or never. "Actually . . ." A pale orange-white fireball forms in them.

I can see his lips lift into a smile.

"What?"

"I always knew you were something special."

I knock my shoulder into him. "You did, did you?"

He laughs, allowing me to pass him. "When Nan asked me to keep an eye on you, I knew that you were more than what you seemed."

"Yes, I am." It's as close to the truth as I'm willing to admit right now.

"Wait," he murmurs, yanking me behind him. The fireball falls from my hands at the sudden motion. He stomps it out with his foot, extinguishing all the light with it.

I hold my breath and wait. In the distance, I hear the faint shuffling of feet against stone. With my eyes closed, my vision travels through the stone wall, down the tunnel until the image of a wolf forms, but not Alaric. A smaller one with glowing yellow eyes.

"It's—" I begin, but Alaric clamps his hand across my mouth again. I think about inserting my thoughts into his mind but decide against it. Revealing small aspects of my true nature piece by piece feels like a much safer, more comfortable approach for both of us. Definitely for me, anyway.

He breathes in, and I know he's seen the same wolf I have. He releases a low rumble that echoes through the walls and to the wolf. It's not a member of his pack. The wolf senses that it's not alone. Instead of running, it welcomes the company. It knows the alpha approaches.

I know I typically embrace denial as if it's my best friend, but really, my best friend is the lone werewolf. I know it.

He begins leading me down the tunnel, and I let him. I will follow him anywhere if it gets me closer to Lizzie. She might want to kill me, but I feel like I'm in pretty good hands.

He stops again. "Wait. There's someone else."

He closes his eyes and breathes in again. I rest my palm against the stone. He has his wolfie ways, and I've got my goddess-magic-witchy-Druid ways.

I try to make out who it is, but the frequency is locked off to me. Clarissa may not have taught me how to block people from my mind, but she did tell me that only powerful practitioners can block me. The fact that someone powerful is meeting my werewolf best friend in the tunnels of the Cathedral, or wherever we've wandered off to, makes me nervous. I reach behind me and pull the dagger from my back pocket.

Alaric pushes it down, shaking his head no.

I touch the wall again but feel nothing but cold stone. They're gone.

"Should we keep going?"

"Yes. One of them was a wolf, and not from my pack."

I try to act surprised with this information. "Who do you think it was?"

"I've caught the scent along the countryside. I've followed it a few times, but I manage to lose it whenever I get to the Cathedral grounds, specifically around Brigit's ruins."

The prison of his father.

"Do you pass by that way often?"

The tunnel is wide enough for us to walk side by side now. "Not usually, but lately I've been drawn to it."

I don't like the sound of that.

"What do you mean, drawn to it?"

"There's something familiar about the place."

I'm sure there is.

And just before the conversation begins to enter into borderline stranger things, we come to a large open cavern/meeting room/creepy place. Our surprise visitors are long gone. I try to get a sense of the energy signature, but it's too blurry in the room. Too much going on.

"Does it seem like this room's been crowded recently?"

He paces around the room. "Yes. Very crowded. With werewolves, and a lot of them."

"What would they be doing down here?"

He stops in front of a wall mural. "I think I can guess."

My gaze follows his. An artist, maybe dozens of artists, carved an entire storyboard into the stone.

"I've never seen anything like it."

"Neither have I," he whispers.

At the top of the mural a large prominent half-man, half-wolf watches over a crowd of half-men, half-wolves. Smaller groups are carved into different segments. Each depicts a part of the werewolf mythology: Clayone's ascent to power, his offer to Derg, the sharing of his blood to spread the werewolf gift, and finally, his people's crippling curses by Brigit. A full moon hovers above them.

There's not one carving hinting at the third curse, that of the nightlock to prevent the change from taking place. I play with a small bundle of it in my pocket—a remnant of the original bundle Gram gave me. The nightlock reassures me that we will be okay. That I'll figure out how to prevent the change.

Based on the weathering of the carvings, they were done a long time ago. Well, all of it with the exception of the image of one large wolf with green eyes standing alone on a hillside watching not only the crowds, but also Clayone. That appears to be a recent addition.

"Clayone," I whisper, my hand following the intricate lines of the carving that represents the Original Werewolf. Here, he cannot harm me or the ones I love.

"You know the story?" Bitterness seeps from open wounds left around his heart. "He used to tell me about the villages he destroyed. The innocent lives lost. The massacres that resulted when legions of new recruits succumbed to their blood lust. He wanted to impress me, to make me want to be like him, but I am nothing like him. That's why I ran away when I knew he was leaving. It wasn't because I didn't want him to leave, it was because I didn't want him to make me go with him. Long ago an angel made sure I didn't need to suffer that werewolf fate of my father. Though she could not reverse what was gifted by another, she could place limitations upon it."

I try to keep breathing in and out to maintain a normal steady human breath, but inside I'm freaking out.

"This looks nothing like her." His hand follows the golden halo above Brigit. He hesitates when he reaches her cheekbones.

"How do you know?"

The Brigit depicted in the carved stone is harsh. Mean. A destroyer of dreams. Nothing like the images I've seen from Clarissa.

He turns to me and lays his hands on either side of my face. "I've spent my life worshiping her in secret. My nan, my auntie, not even my dad knew. She came to me many times, in many different forms, but this one I like the most of all."

He ducks down and kisses me.

Clapping echoes through the space. "Bravo on the mutual discovery. As for the setting . . ." Breas says, stalking toward us, "I would have chosen better. I have chosen better."

Alaric lunges at him.

Breas throws up his hand and Alaric smashes into an invisible shield, which knocks him backward.

"I don't think so . . ." Breas laughs.

Alaric leaps up and launches himself at Breas again. Breas jerks his fist and twists. "I'm ready for you this time."

Alaric's body twists in the same motion before smashing against the floor.

"Stop," I scream. "Please stop."

But neither one of them listens. Alaric struggles back to a standing position before lunging again. Breas thrusts out his hand, fingers spread out. Alaric stops with it, hovering in the air.

"Our first meeting I was not prepared for whom I would be dealing with, but now . . ." Breas raises his fist. Alaric rises with it, and then Breas swings his arm down and Alaric crashes to the floor.

"Stop, please stop," I sob.

Alaric tries again and again to rise, but Breas smashes him against the stone floor each time.

I can't watch anymore of it. It has to end. "Stop," I scream. "Breas, stop."

Breas turns to me and smiles before knocking Alaric into the mural wall.

"I'll do anything if you stop," I cry.

He looks at me. "Anything?"

"Gi, no," Alaric mumbles.

Breas flicks his wrist. Alaric's eyes bulge out of his head. He gasps for breath.

"You're choking him! Breas, stop. I'll do anything you ask. Just stop."

"If you insist," he says, twisting his arm. Alaric goes still.

From where I stand across the room, he looks dead. I'm paralyzed to move.

"Did you kill him?" I whisper, tears streaming down my cheeks.

"No," he says, "but I will if you don't do as I ask."

He has me exactly where he wants me. "What do you want from me?"

He smiles his cruel Joker smile that makes me want to vomit. If I wasn't so broken, I would.

"You're going to take him and lock him in there," he says, pointing to what appears to be a cell. "When you're done, you're going to join me and help return my people to their land."

"Your people?"

He winks at me. "You'll get no more from me until the stars align with the moon in their proper position at their appointed time."

"Why not take what you want from me now? Why keep me as a prisoner when you can rid yourself of me?"

He stalks over, wraps his hand around my neck, and wrenches me to him. "Don't think I haven't thought about it. But alas, you're far too valuable to eliminate. He, on the other hand," he says, releasing me, "I will rid the world of him just as I've done in each lifetime you've managed to find one another."

Heat flickers in my palms. Clarissa told me I couldn't injure another living being with my magic, but what about a god? Can I hurt him for all the times he's hurt me and, evidently, Alaric?

I should think so, but wait until you can protect your love.

"Why would you do that?"

He lunges at me. "Why?"

I scurry backward. He feints to the right. I swerve to the left, but he's expecting me. He yanks me to him. "You are mine. You will always be mine. Now, chain him." He throws me at Alaric. I stumble across the floor toward him.

He flings heavy chains at me, and I jump out of the way to avoid them. When I grasp the cold chains, heat begins to radiate through them. Soon the metal glows red.

"Hurry," he snarls, sounding more like a beast than a man. "I haven't got all day."

Strength and courage blossom within me. He will pay for messing with someone I care about.

"Oh, Breas," I sing out to him.

He stomps toward me. "What?"

"Catch!" and I hurl the white-hot chains at his head. They wrap around his upper body like a snake. While he's wrapped in them, I throw my hands at him again and again, bombarding him with fireballs. He screams for mercy, but rather than stop, I continue attacking him until blood splatters across his face.

I soon realize the blood is from the wound on my palm. I clench it to me as I whirl around, searching for Alaric, but he's not where Breas left him.

He's gone.

He'd never leave me, and he's in no condition to leave on his own. Someone took him. I'll find out who soon enough. First, I've got an asshole to deal with.

The cell where Breas wanted to imprison Alaric seemed the appropriate place to stash away a god who was once my husband. If I wasn't so sure he knew Lizzie's whereabouts, I'd let him rot in there for an eternity, but he possesses valuable information, so for now, I need to wait until he reveals her location.

A simple cloaking spell will keep him hidden from anyone who passes by the cell. Only I will know his true location, and I will not be sharing that with anyone.

Especially Scott. He gets squeamish when it comes to prolonged torture. I, however, am looking forward to it.

I never dreamed that my second wish after waking from the seomra de rúin would come true, and by proximity, my third wish—to find and save Lizzie. But in his current condition, Breas is of no use to me. I might have overdone it with the fireball volley.

He deserves much worse.

"So much for peace-loving goddess," I say to myself.

You don't know what he did.

"So, show me."

Let him.

I stand outside the cell, gripping the bars, staring at his collapsed frame. I've been in his mind before. I don't relish doing it again. I take a deep breath to ground myself to this plane, then focus on his mind.

The wind whips through my hair as I speed back to town, back to people who worship me. Kensey will give me what I want tonight. She treats me as I deserve to be treated.

I bank the bike, just missing the tree on the tight curve again. The ghost of her arms still clings to my waist. It was my intent to drive her back to me, but it appears that I've added to the wall between us instead.

She deserves to freeze to death. The portal is feet away from her, and she can't even sense it. The stupid whore. How dare she deny me what is so rightfully mine? The blocking magic they've laid upon her is far heavier than I suspected. Far more than the witch warned me about.

I grow stronger every day just being near her. Soon I will have enough power of my own to open the portal. Soon I will set my plan into action.

A lone figure in a white dress walks down the middle of the street. Wind whips her hair across her face as if a mighty storm blew in, but the night sky is filled only with stars. As I approach the barefoot figure, she raises her arms, palms open, fingers wide. I slide to a stop in front of her and remove my helmet.

"Breas, you disappoint me," Lizzie says, though she doesn't sound like herself.

"And how do I disappoint you? Because, evidently, I cannot satisfy your best friend."

She clucks her tongue. "Come now, you don't recognize me?"

I peer into soulless black eyes and realize to whom I am speaking. "How did you possess her?"

She smiles. "I am more than a conjuror of gods."

"Have you taken full possession?"

"I haven't. When she's around Brigit, it is difficult to maintain control. She's merely a vessel to ensure you have fulfilled your obligations."

I wrap my hand around her throat. "And what obligations might that be? Am I not a god?"

She fights to pry my fingers lose. She gasps, "She is a vessel. If you kill her, I'll just find another."

I squeeze. I watch the blackness slip from her eyes, and the amber gold returns. "Breas," she coughs, "Breas, what are you doing?" She claws at my arms.

"Honor me," I order her and keep squeezing.

She gasps, "I honor you. I honor you."

I release her, and she collapses to the pavement, her hands clutching her throat. I watch her chest rise and fall as she tries to catch her breath. It is in that moment I make a decision. I swoop down and nestle her into my chest. "Come now, darling, 'tis all right. Let me tuck you into bed. Your memories of this evening will be nothing more than a bad dream, and I will be your hero."

"That is a lovely story," she croaks.

I smile to myself. The witch will not win a game in which I am the master.

. . .

The night he almost killed me on the motorcycle, he strangled Lizzie. He wanted to get rid of the witch who evidently took up residence in Lizzie for an extended holiday. Was it the next day Lizzie, a.k.a. The Witch, went all mean-girl-psycho-séance-scene on Kensey? A witch possession would explain why Lizzie tried to sacrifice Kensey, or whatever sinister plot she had planned in the attic.

He mentioned a witch powerful enough to work her evil magic from a distance—magic I now realize was Maleficium. Carman sent Alaric to watch me. She must have possessed Lizzie through that freaky eyeball necklace. It wasn't until I buried it deep in the woods behind Gram's house that Lizzie returned to herself.

Then everything shifts clearly into focus.

Carman opened the portal for Breas. She sent Clayone. She possessed Lizzie. Her evil contaminated everything it touched.

Not everything. Not Alaric.

And now he's gone.

I yank at the bars of the cell, wanting to bend them to my will and wrap Breas up in them. I may not be endowed with physical strength like Scott, but there are other types of strength. Before I exact my revenge on Breas, however, I need to know where Lizzie is. I relax my grip and reach a hand through, close my eyes, and focus on extracting Lizzie's whereabouts.

Since my arrival I've wanted to kiss her. I've yearned for her soft, sweet petals since the battle. For that night, it was not her lips I desired.

The battle served two purposes. Sate Derg's lust for blood—though the God of Death will never be satisfied until every last drop of blood has seeped into his hungry mouth. The other? Obtain the Vessel of Life.

I gasp and open my eyes, bringing me out of his head.

Keep going.

I tighten my grip on the bars to further ground myself, before I reach my left hand back through to delve deeper into his mind.

Gaping wounds flowed rivers of blood. The crows had already begun to devour the soft flesh. I stood watching as a silvery white light descended upon the water. The air shimmered, and she stepped through the opening of the portal onto the field strewn with bodies.

As she took in the wreckage, tears began to stream down her face. A loud, shrill sound arose from her chest. Her keening could be heard for miles, but there was no one who could protect her. I had made sure of that.

I always thought her weak for her love of the humans, but it proved a useful war strategy. She clutched the Vessel of Life to her chest with one hand as she weaved in and out of the bodies. She stretched her free arm out across the field with her eyes closed, searching for life.

If she hoped to find any, she was mistaken. Those who didn't die from loss of blood, turned to stone.

When the air shifted, she stiffened. She caught my scent amongst the stench of rotting bodies.

I moved with haste, pulling the sword high above my head. I swung it in a wide arc mere inches from her throat. The heavy cauldron crashed with a loud thud upon a stone-hardened body. She ducked and rolled out of the blade's reach.

She took one last look at me before she leapt through the portal opening, leaving the Vessel behind.

Betrayal mired her features then, as it does now, along with the hate she cannot explain the reason for. In her current form, she remembers not what happened the day of the battle, but the hate and betrayals linger, as does the lust—and that I will use to my benefit.

Soon my plan will be set into motion, and the Vessel of Life will be put to its full potential.

I pull out of his mind. The iron bars between us are white hot, even with only one hand holding them. I release my grip so as not to weaken them. Breas needs to pay for his crimes against humanity, but now he is in possession of two things I need.

Scott warned me about tampering with my soul to bring back the ones we loved, but what if Breas were to do it? What if I could coerce him into bringing them all back? I don't care about his soul. He barely has any left anyway. I'll just take what remains.

Careful not to touch the iron, I poke a hand back through and close my eyes. I probe around with a singular focus on the Vessel of Life, but his mind is blank. He's completely expended tonight, and so am I. I need to recharge before I search for Lizzie and Alaric. Their lives depend on it.

I leave Breas to recover from his wounds because tomorrow is another day, and I've got some fun things planned for him.

Scott runs over to me when I enter the cottage. "What happened to you? Where have you been?"

Given my current state of disaster—holey jeans, ripped

shirt, tear-stained face, missing boyfriend, missing best friend once possessed by the most powerful Maleficium witch that ever existed and now a werewolf BFF—he's definitely not overreacting.

I slump into the nearest chair, the day taking its toll like a freaking stone wall smashed over my head—oh, wait, that's what happened to Alaric. "Where do I even begin?"

He crouches in front of me. "From the beginning."

"In the beginning Breas and Brigit were husband and wife."

He falls back on his butt. "What?"

"For some reason, and I don't know why, I married Breas, or at least the Goddess Brigit did. I think I agreed to do it in order to settle a war in hopes of peace."

"What war?"

I shake my head. "I don't know."

"To join the Tuatha Dé Danann and the Fomorians together," Granda says from his bedroom doorway.

Scott's forehead scrunches. "Them again? What's their deal anyway?"

"They were the early inhabitants of Ireland. Your people."

Scott narrows his gaze. "You and Clarissa and Gigi are my people. Dad and Gram were my people."

Granda sits down in the chair beside me. He looks much better than he did this afternoon, but he still aged today. The energy demanded of him will never be recovered. "The Tuatha Dé Danann are our gods. The Fomorians were the predecessors to them like the Titans to the Greek gods. The Tuatha Dé Danann ruled Ireland for many years, and the Fomorians wanted to take back what was once theirs."

Another group wanting what someone else had. Big freaking surprise there. "And what did they want?"

"The land above the water."

Granda's not really providing two ignorant reincarnated gods much information to work with.

"And the Fomorians lived . . ."

"Under the water."

"Fins, gills, scales?" Scott counts them off on his fingers.

"More like ferocious, vicious, and bloodthirsty."

Let's get to the most important matter at hand. "And a marriage to Breas ended the war?"

"More or less."

"Why?"

"Tuatha Dé Danann cherished perfection above all else. Breas was their king until he fell from favor when he failed to properly shelter and feed a bard."

Scott leans forward. "A what?"

"A bard. A poet. A storyteller."

We continue circling around the meat of it. "And why did they stop liking him? Aside from the many reasons I don't."

"Because of his inhospitable treatment of his guest, the bard told the story to the first person he met, and because he was a Druid, his words were magic. The story proliferated throughout Ireland. It was considered a grievous aspect of the king's nature. Breas was no longer perfect in the eyes of his people and, therefore, could no longer be their king.

"With the absence of a strong leader, the Tuatha Dé Danann splintered into factions. The Fomorians took advantage of this unrest, and small skirmishes began breaking out. Breas went to Brigit, beloved daughter of Anu and Dagda and cherished among all the Tuatha Dé Danann, knowing a union with her would ensure his position as ruler. Brigit did not love him, but in order to stop the killing, she agreed.

"Peace prevailed, but not as long as one would expect. The tides began to shift, and the Tuatha Dé Danann were getting murdered at night in their beds. The bloodshed continued. Breas planned the Battle of Moytura to end the fighting. On the battlefield, something happened to Brigit, but no one knows what, for not one person survived. Breas returned as king, but his seat on the throne did not last long after Brigit's disappearance."

"I know what happened," I hiss.

"Gigi, what do you mean? I assumed you didn't possess any memories of the Goddess," Granda says, nodding toward my hands.

I squeeze them together, extinguishing the fireballs. It seems that every time I get angry now, fireballs erupt. Given my propensity for it, I might wind up igniting the world. "Breas slaughtered every person on that field in order to lure Brigit there."

Scott shifts in his seat. He doesn't like hearing about bad things happening to anyone, and he hates people capable of such atrocities. "Why would he murder people to get his wife to show up?"

"Oh my god, I can't believe I didn't realize it sooner." Granda smacks the side of his head. "There were only rumors, suspicions, but no one wanted to believe that even a fallen king would betray hundreds of people. Now we know . . . he wanted the Vessel of Life."

Just add a new layer of self-loathing right here. "And I gave it to him like a fucking idiot."

He lays his hand across mine. "The two of you were bound together. You trusted him. You didn't know his intentions. He kept his true nature hidden from you and his people. No one has known what happened that day for thousands of years."

Scott turns to me. He's not suspicious, but he's well aware that I haven't shared everything swirling around in my mind. "How did you find this out? Do you have any memory of him before Vernal Falls?"

I haven't shared with Scott or anyone else that I've slipped into Breas's mind, nor about my dreams that must have been visions back in Vernal Falls. And honestly, it's not important. Nobody needs to know that shit. Besides, most of what I learned reinforces that Breas's been a rat bastard since the beginning of his existence. He is the King of Bullshit though—I'll give him that.

Scott also won't appreciate that I went all psycho-bitch on him, even when I had the Goddess's blessings. He judges.

"Well, here's the thing . . ." I begin, and even if I couldn't read Scott's mind, it's clear by the tilt of his head and the jerk of his lip, that he's thinking, Here we go. "There's a secret tunnel from the Cathedral library to a creepy-ass dungeon."

Granda jerks forward. "What? Where? I'm only familiar with one, and it connects the first and second floor of the Cathedral. I've heard rumors, sure, but I've never discovered it. Where is it?"

I have nothing to hide from Granda or Scott in this case. Secret tunnel locations ought to be fully disclosed. "In the farthest corner of the library, in the old books section, there's a tapestry of Brigit holding a candle in one hand and a plant in the other. The secret tunnel is behind that."

Granda shakes his head in disbelief. "Impossible. I personally rehung that tapestry twenty years ago. I assure you, there is no secret passageway behind it."

"I assure you that there is. And based on the carvings Alaric and I found in a large cavern meeting room, it's been around for a very long time. And judging by its off-the-charts energy signatures, a lot of people use it regularly."

"What were you doing with Alaric? You said you were going to the library for research."

Nothing matches Scott's dull-pointed accusations. They really stab you between the eyes and leave you itchy and annoyed. "I did go to the library for research. Alaric showed up."

He rests against the back of his chair. "Yeah, right."

"Maria showed up too."

He straightens. "Really? Why? What did she say?"

"We don't have to time to talk about your love life right now. Alaric is missing."

Granda waves his hands in front of me. "Hold on. We're getting way off topic. One thing at a time, starting with the most important: the missing Vessel of Life." He pauses and reconsiders. "Not that a missing beau isn't important, but the Vessel of Life vanished thousands of years ago."

And the bitch comes out to play with her claws sharpened. "Right, I get it. What's one missing werewolf, even if he is Gigi's boyfriend."

"I didn't say that. But if the Vessel of Life were to get into the wrong hands, the consequences could be severe."

Scott clasps his hands together. "Just how severe are we talking? A potential army of immortal werewolves who could change whenever the mood hit them seemed pretty darn severe to me."

Granda folds his hands together and presses them against his lips, deep in thought. Typically I don't have much patience to work with, but with Lizzie and Alaric's lives on the line, I've got none. I'm about snap when he finally says, "I'd really like Clarissa here so we can discuss it together, but alas, it's the middle of the night, and time is passing. It's been long suspected that Breas's father was not his mother's husband, but rather a man from an enemy faction."

I tuck my hands under my legs to keep them from sparking. "And that enemy faction might be . . ."

"The Fomorians."

Scott waves his hands. "Hold up. Wasn't Breas the king of the Tuatha Dé Danann?"

"Yes, but many believed that his father was a Fomorian. His mother was known to consort with them. When his power was threatened following the bard fiasco, he could have sought annihilation of the invading Fomorians by his armies and gained back the respect of his people. Instead he—"

"Instead he tricked Brigit into joining with him in order to get the Vessel of Life," I finish.

"Thus ensuring that when he was ready to lift the veil between the worlds, he could bring back from the dead the legions of Fomorians he had slaughtered and, by sheer numbers, his position as king."

Scott refuses to allow his mind to go where Granda and mine leapt so easily. "That is a horrific fairy tale myth, but in contemporary times Ireland has a prime minister, and a parliament. How does some egomaniac become ruler of a country in a world inundated by rules and elections and millions of people?"

"By eliminating them," Granda replies.

Scott searches for a loophole to prevent Granda's theory from being possible. "Yes, well, aren't there bodyguards and security and hundreds of other measures to ensure that an overthrow doesn't occur? And wouldn't a neighboring country come to Ireland's assistance if they went under domestic attack?"

Granda shakes his head. "Not if he manages to bring Balor, the most terrible Fomorian, back from the dead."

It's my turn to throw my hands up in the air. "Balor? Okay, please, please don't tell me that he's some freaky grandfather werewolf who can kill hundreds of people in one sitting."

"No. Much worse."

Scott smacks the side of his head. "There could be worse?"

"Are you familiar with the story of Medusa?"

Scott refuses to say another word—he's heard far too much already—but I figure, ripping off the bandage stings like the holy mother, at least the worst is over. "Snake pets in her hair, turns people to stone if they look at her, kick-ass archer. She's real?"

"Well, yes, she is, but take her power and inject it into one eyeball that requires four men to lift the eyelid using a giant iron ring. Then, once it's open, every living thing the eyeball falls upon turns to stone. One gaze and . . ."

"Complete annihilation," I finish for him. I hate that I can finish his thoughts. Especially given the topic. "We need to get that Vessel."

Scott embraces his cynicism. He normally keeps it locked away, but it busts out. "What about Alaric? Aren't you worried about him? I thought he was your great love or something."

He's trying to grasp this new information that Granda shared with us. He's not trying to be cruel intentionally. Well, I guess he is, but when the actual destruction of the world and every living thing on it is a very real possibility, I believe he's entitled. "Alaric and I have lived many lives together. And maybe he will be my great love in this one, but right now, humanity's survival seems a tad more important."

"When you put it that way, I sound like a real shallow dick. I wanted to find out if Maria asked about me." A smile emerges, and he locks his crazy-ass side back up. "How will we find this Vessel of Life? We don't even know where Breas is staying."

I wave my finger. "Actually, I can help with that."

"How did I know you were going to say that?"

"He might be locked in a cell in the dungeon Alaric and I found."

"Why would he be anyplace else?"

"He might have some injuries."

"Right. Injuries. I'd expect nothing less. I thought you were unable to injure another living being."

"Turns out that doesn't apply to backstabbing god husbands."

"Lucky for you."

"Quite."

And the two reincarnated gods venture out into the night, ready to kick some major god ass.

MISPLACED GODS

*N*either of us speaks as we wind our way through the tunnels, so you know we are on a serious mission. I mean, we aren't just talking about immortal werewolves anymore, we're dealing with the potential end of the world as we know it. After we masterminded the true nature of Breas's diabolical plan, Scott bolstered my energy. He is vital to my existence, and now, we're going to wake up Breas and find out everything he knows. It's going to be a real brother-sister bonding experience.

When we get to the cavern meeting room, Scott sees the wall carving depicting Clayone along with the werewolf mythology. He sees the lone wolf on top of the hill observing everything. He doesn't say anything about it, but I know he's figured out it's Alaric, and as much as he wants to trust him for my sake, he can't do it. Not yet anyway.

When we approach Breas's cell, there is a white-haired woman sitting on the floor.

"Clarissa, what are you doing here?"

Clarissa glares up at me, then Scott, then points to the cell. "I could ask you the same question."

We peek through the bars, both with the assumption she's referring to Breas, but the cell's empty.

"What happened to him?"

She crosses her arms. "I was going to ask you the same thing."

"He was in that cell, curled up in a ball. I cloaked him so no one could find him."

She pushes herself up from the floor to glare at me some more. "It appears someone did."

"I can see that. But how?"

"Are you certain you were alone?"

"Yes."

Are you certain?

"No. No, I'm not."

Scott pushes between us. "Gigi, what's going on?"

I fling out my arms in dramatic effect. "Breas is missing along with our only link to Lizzie or the Vessel of Life."

Clarissa grabs my hands. "Are you certain he has the Vessel of Life?"

I close my eyes and show her.

"Oh," she gasps, releasing me.

"No shit," Scott mumbles. "But what happened to him? Is it that same person that took Alaric and Lizzie?"

"Alaric is missing as well?"

"I thought you could see the future. That's how you found us, isn't it?"

She gestures for us to follow her farther down the hallway. "In some cases, yes, but I also have a phone. We're not in the Middle Ages."

"Granda called you?"

She winks. "No, actually, your presence flickered a few hours ago. I tracked your essence here via an energy locator spell."

I check my arms and legs, searching for a foreign object. "You put a tracker on me?"

"No, not an actual tracker, but it might have been a tracker spell."

"You took some of my hair when I was in the seomra de rúin, didn't you." I narrow my eyes at her. She tries not to look guilty, but she doesn't succeed. "You'd think after fifteen hundred years you would have mastered lying or at least hiding the truth."

"I didn't take it today. I took it from your hairbrush when you first arrived."

Scott laughs at the both of us. "Gi, I think you've met your match."

Clarissa stops in front of another set of cells ahead of us.

"I guess so. But why are we still down here? If Breas isn't here, what more do we need?"

She points in another cell. "Take a look."

Scott and I peek inside. This cell's also empty, but there are chains with locks scattered around the perimeter of the cell."

"What was this place?" Scott whispers.

I stare at the claw marks all over the floor, the walls, the bars. I hurry to the next cell and the one after that, and they are all the same. I swallow hard, unable to believe what we've found.

Scott braces himself. He knows he's not going to like what I tell him, but I have to tell him anyway. "What is this place, Gi?"

"It's where Carman experimented on werewolves. She must have spent centuries working to perfect the werewolf." I think about Alaric and his goodness and my faith that he wasn't capable of hurting me, and then I remember how he told me sometimes he woke up and he was covered with blood and mud, and he didn't know where it came from . . .

In daylight he is yours.
In the deepest night he belongs to another.
Divided, he will break.
United, he will destroy that which tried to
    break him.

The wolves will come for me. They will come for me and kill me. I betrayed their leader by allowing him to be taken. I betrayed them all. And they seek retribution.

They want my blood, and so they shall have it.

I let the realization fall over me like armor, but even an impenetrable fortress will not save me from what I've done. I bear this responsibility fully and without consequence. When I die, the wolves will gnaw at my bones, and the cycle will begin again.

The daylight was mine. The moonlight belonged to another.

And I wanted all of it.

DARK MOON SPELL WORK

Scott lights his sage bundle from the red candle representing fire. "Do you really think we should be doing this when everything's gone to shit?"

I continue pouring salt around the boundary of the circle. "Sure, why not? What harm could we possibly cause?"

He shifts the chalice of water into the western corner. "I could think of a few dozen."

"Yeah, well, with Breas missing we need to find the Vessel of Life as soon as possible. And Lizzie. And since I'm feeling greedy, Alaric too."

"You miss him, don't you."

I breathe in and out of my nose and finish the circle. It's not a weakness to admit you care about someone—I have to remember that. "Yeah, I do."

I haven't told Scott that I know the wolves are planning to kill me. He's got enough to worry about. And whether they can actually kill me or not, I really don't know. Not that I'm too anxious to find out, but what can you do? The world and every living being is running out of time, and I need to get my Vessel back.

"Do you think Granda and Clarissa know what we're doing?" He doesn't sound nervous so much as worried what they might think of him. If they do know, they didn't mention it.

Since Breas's disappearance, they've been working on finding the Vessel of Life. Their coven has searched every house along the coast, and as of yet they haven't found the Irish ding-dong. It appears he knows his own cloaking spells and, evidently, how to uncloak mine or he would not have been found in the dungeon in the first place.

Scott hands me the second bowl of crystals. The first bowl is in the northern corner to represent Earth. This one I'll imbue with nightlock. Any werewolf who wears one of these crystals won't change on the full moon. Or at least that's what's supposed to happen, but we all know how my life plans work out. The idea came from my very own crystal necklace that I got from Clarissa.

"How are we going to get the wolves to wear the crystals? Hand them out at a festival? Host a bonfire the night before the full moon and give out crystal necklace party favors?"

I smudge my sage bundle in another bowl—one of Gram's pottery ones. I feel a closer connection with her that way. "I haven't worked out the finer details of that part. It seems like taking life day by day is a better plan for me."

"Gi, you've got me to protect you."

"I'm not sure a mini tornado qualifies as assistance."

"Always with the comeback."

Scott's been focusing on grounding his magic, so he hasn't had any explosions since that first one.

I glance up at the night sky. The Dark Moon phase lasts less than twenty-four hours. Midday is a powerful time, but midnight is the most powerful. I shift the bowl of crystals with the crushed nightlock over the fire. "Are you ready?"

"Ready as I'll ever be."

We take turns calling to each of the elements. Each time we work spells together, our spell work evolves and changes. We always find our own method and pattern.

"To the Dark Moon, I ask for your blessing of the crystals, for they are powerful in their own right, but when imbued with nightlock, the wolf will no longer be forced to shift into its animal form. Still powerful. Still being. But their thirst for blood will be quenched. They will not be forced to kill to feed. They will not give in to their appetite on the full moon but will still be sated." I stir the crystals with a wooden spoon and mix the nightlock through it. I chant a few more lines, then pass my hands over the bowl, forcing my energy into them. They begin to glow a deep purple.

"Look at that," Scott whispers. "It's happening."

The crystals grow brighter and brighter, glowing in the Dark Moon night. The nightlock turns to liquid and then disappears into the crystals. When all the liquid is gone, the crystals fade, eventually becoming clear again.

I take a crystal from the bowl and hold it over the fire so I can examine it. The faint hint of purple tells me that their transformation was successful.

Scott's hand hovers close by. He's afraid to touch them and mess them up. "Did it work?"

I drop it in his hand. "It did."

"Wow," he murmurs. "That was cool."

"You realize that was the easy part, right?"

He sighs, putting it back in the bowl. "I know. What's next?"

I lay out my hand for him. "Dagger?"

He reaches down and removes it from his leg strap. "Dagger."

"Cut me," I whisper.

"Gi, no."

"Cut me. It's the only way."

He's reluctant for a number of reasons, one being that he's always sworn to protect me.

"You will be protecting me by doing this."

"Fine. Hold still." He takes my hand and drags the blade across it. I barely feel a thing.

"Do you sharpen that thing?"

"No," he says, cleaning it with the rag he brought for such an occasion—he's such a clean freak. Once blood-free, he returns it to his leg strap.

I hold my cut palm over another bowl and the blood begins to drip. When the first drop of blood hits the bowl, the wind picks up outside the circle.

He looks up at the sky. "Real or supernatural?"

"I don't know, but let's hurry. I probably need a few more drops to begin the locator spell."

With every drop, the wind picks up, getting stronger and stronger. After the third drop, a rumble of thunders shakes the ground.

"Gi, I think we should stop."

I shake my head and squeeze for more blood to fall. "No. We need to keep going."

A lightning strike hits next to the circle. "That was close," he says. "Gi, we need to stop."

Freezing rain pelts our faces as wind whips across the field. "No, it's fine."

"Gi . . ."

"Can't you do something? Like counteract it with a mini tornado?"

"Gi, I . . ."

I flick my hand at him. He winces as if I'd actually smacked his face.

Maybe I did.

"What was that for?"

"Just try. Ground yourself like Clarissa told you to."

He tries to focus on the air and the wind. While he's occupied, I chant a locator spell I made up based on the spell book I found, Dad's journal, and a few other books from the Cathedral library. It's a mishmash of magic, but I think it'll work. It has to.

The more I chant, the harder the wind gets. I envision the large iron cauldron. I form the copper handles in my mind. I reach out my arms for the Vessel of Life and ask it to come to me.

Hail starts pelting my face. I wince as I keep chanting with my outstretched hands.

"Gigi, we need to stop. It's not safe for you out here."

I ignore him and keep chanting. Another flash of lightning strikes, this time three feet away from me. Static electricity rushes through me.

"The circle—it's disappearing in the rain," he screams.

"Focus, Scott. Please try. Please!"

He struggles with the fear welling up inside of him. Fear for my well-being, fear for the world, and fear of the storm because some scary-ass shit is going on.

He throws out his hands and stretches himself physically and mentally. It's a sight to behold, and I temporarily forget what I'm doing. Then I remember.

I chant while he chants, but now, instead of a quiet, steady chant, our words are loud, impatient screams.

A steam engine winds its way toward us. The noise is deafening. When my ears feel like they will explode, everything stops. The rain, the sleet, the thunder, the lighting, the wind—everything.

I feel the lightest fairy wing kiss of a touch in my outstretched hand before it disappears.

"You did it," Scott whispers.

I open my eyes to look at the goblet in my hand.

"No, I didn't. It's not the Vessel of Life."

"What is it then?"

"The Chalice of Healing."

"Wow," he says in awe. "That's amazing. Is that what you used on me?"

All of a sudden the stillness bursts with birdsong. I look over at Scott. Four birds are circling above his head. I keep my mouth shut, but I can't help laughing.

"Don't say it," he says. "Don't."

"You made fun of my cows. At least they plowed Clayone into my chambers and helped me seal him away for all eternity. You bring four little tweety birds to save us? Really?"

"Their song is very soothing."

"I agree, it is, but you've got bird shit on your shoulder."

He hunches his shoulders up, swinging his head back and forth. "Which one?"

I shake my head. "You are so easy."

"Okay, thank you," he says, waving them away. As they disappear into the night and we're left in the silence that follows, he turns to me.

"What's next?"

I clutch the Chalice of Healing to my chest. "I'll hold onto this. You grab those," I tell him, pointing to the nightlock-imbued crystals.

We start our long walk home.

"And what do we do about Breas, the Vessel of Life, and Balor?"

"Well, if the voice in my head is any indication, Breas won't be able to open a portal or create a rip between the worlds until there's a full moon and the stars align in a certain celestial pattern that no one but ultimate space nerds and evil villains seem to know, along with some seismic shift caused by an earthquake in some far-off country on the other side of the world."

"And when will that be?"

I sigh. "Well, I don't know when, but I'm sure Granda would love the opportunity to consult his books and his astrological space nerd buddies."

"Do you think they're actually aliens?"

I laugh. "After everything, after discovering that all kinds of monsters and gods go bump in the night, maybe."

"What's next for us?"

"Well, if we last two weeks in this realm, we start our training in the Shadow Realm."

"As long as we're together, we'll get through this."

"You got that right."

THE END

REVIEWS ARE LIKE DANCE PARTIES. SOMEONE HAS
TO GET THEM STARTED!

Continue reading for an excerpt of SHADOW MOON: THE
GODDESS CHRONICLES BOOK 4

JOIN THE KOVEN

Read Clarissa and Carman's origin story, The Druids Sisters of the Gallicennial, FREE by signing up for K's Koven. Be the FIRST to find out about new releases from Best-Selling Author, K.B. Anne. PLUS, receive <u>Newsletter Subscriber</u> Only Bonus Content, insight on Celtic Mythology, Druids, Witches, Werewolves, and Magic, and so much more! <u>Join K's Koven</u> today!

The Goddess Chronicles (COMPLETE)

Wide Awake: The Goddess Chronicles Book 1

Blood Moon: The Goddess Chronicles Book 2

Dark Moon: The Goddess Chronicles Book 3

Shadow Moon: The Goddess Chronicles Book 4

Oak Moon: The Goddess Chronicles Book 5

Storm Moon: The Goddess Chronicles Book 6

The Goddess Chronicles Books 1-3 Boxset

The Goddess Chronicles Books 4-6 Boxset

The Silver Fae Series (COMPLETE)

Throne of Silver: Silver Fae 1

Silver Fae Hunter: Silver Fae 2

Heirs of Wings and Shadows: Silver Fae 3

Court of Wings and Shadows: Silver Fae 4

Crown of Flames: Silver Fae 5

ABOUT THE AUTHOR

Evil author person causing book hangovers since 2018. Known to erupt into malevolent laughter fits while she writes urban fantasy featuring fierce females, swoon worthy heroes who actually listen, and explosive action because everyone needs excitement in their lives.

She writes the best-selling urban fantasy series, *The Goddess Chronicles* and *The Silver Fae* Series. She has a thing for drool worthy wolf shapeshifters. Who doesn't?

She lives in Northeast PA with 3 goblins, a task master, 2 hell hound overlords, and 2 unicorns—though sadly they don't fart rainbow glitter. The Goddess Chronicles and Silver Fae Series are ready for your consumption. Warning: May cause book hangovers.

Visit her website for more information or to contact her at kbanne.com.

Contact info:
www.KBAnne.com
kim@kbanne.com

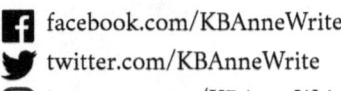 facebook.com/KBAnneWrite
twitter.com/KBAnneWrite
instagram.com/KBAnneWrite

SHADOW MOON: THE GODDESS CHRONICLES BOOK 4

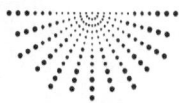

PROLOGUE

*T*he throne room was forbidden to Caer on this eve of Samhain, and she didn't understand why. As princess, she should have unrestricted movement throughout the castle, coming and going as she pleased just like she did at all times—well, with the exception of her nursemaid following her about, though Caer was talented at losing her. But alas, her father forbade her from entering it tonight.

She thought it cruel of her father and unforgiveable. She'd find another way in to watch the unexpected guests, especially on this most auspicious of nights.

Once, long ago, she had overheard her nursemaid talk about secret tunnels that wound their way behind the rooms and hallways of the castle. They led to underground dungeons full of monsters that would turn even the strongest of the guards to greasy pools of cowardice if not for the powerful magic cast upon them by her father's trusted Druid.

She had stalked around the castle, pressing on stones, hovering her hand over cracks in the mortar, and sometimes kicking the impenetrable rock in hopes that she'd find her way to the secret tunnels. She'd had no intention of sneaking into the dungeons. Those monsters were best kept away from people. But the tunnels? Well, that was a temptation she couldn't resist.

She'd searched for the tunnels through most of the castle, patiently and painstakingly for many moons, until find them she did. The fates finally blessed her the night of Samhain. Earlier that afternoon her nursemaid had discovered Caer skulking around the castle in search of the tunnels and had punished the princess for her unsupervised wanderings by sending her to bed long before sunset. In a fit of anger and desperation, Caer sought to block the entrance to her room by shoving the dresser away from the long tapestry that had hung from her wall since birth. That was when she found the tunnel entrance at last.

Caer grabbed the torch off the wall and pushed the loose stone in. The creaking of wood pulleys and the grinding of stone against stone followed before the "door" appeared. Without a backward glance, she crept into the tunnel, shutting the door and her only known exit behind her.

She trod carefully along the musty passage, trying not to sneeze from the dust and mold. The bitter cold raised goosebumps on her arms. She wished she'd grabbed a shawl, but it was too late now. The Samhain ceremony would begin when the moon became visible in the night sky. She'd do without warmth if she wished to watch the festivities.

At each intersection, she closed her eyes and pictured the corridors that ran parallel to the tunnels. Based on her sense of direction she'd turn left or right, pacing off the length of the hallways she had traveled ever since her legs had been able to teeter down them. She wound her way through the castle, confident that she was heading in the right direction. But when she didn't arrive at the throne room when she thought she should, she began to doubt herself. Her father's castle was large, especially compared to the other castles she'd visited when she was younger, but still the throne room couldn't be much farther. If the tunnels went any deeper underground, she'd wind up discovering the dungeons, and she didn't have the stomach for real-life monsters. The ones in her imagination were enough.

When she was sure that Derg himself would open the gates to the Underworld for her, she heard footsteps thundering on stone. She knew her father had one guest in particular that he didn't want her to see—she suspected he was the main reason she wasn't allowed into the throne room that evening—but it sounded like hordes of guests were participating in the ceremony tonight. All the more reason to hurry.

A narrow shaft of light broke through from the stone wall and hit the opposite one. She listened first, priding herself on her patience and cautionary discretion. When it seemed that no one was standing on the other side of the peephole, she leaned toward it. She could barely see through the opening, but that didn't stop her from trying. Her father sat on his throne. In front of him stood the one she presumed was his honored guest. The one he didn't want Caer to meet.

He stood taller than any man she'd ever seen, including Percy and Roman, her father's most formidable personal guards. Her father smiled tightly at the guest—out of character for him. The King was known as a most hospitable host, and his reputation grew each time an enchanted bard came to visit. But this beast of a man was no bard. Even Percy and Roman seemed to shrink away from him.

"He must be deformed in some way," she whispered to herself. It was the only explanation for her father's cold greeting.

As if the man knew she was hiding on the other side of the wall, he spun on his heel to face her. Gasping, she jumped away from her peephole. A large leather patch covered one of his eyes. She had heard of pirates that raided ships and raped and pillaged. The giant must be one. But why had her father invited him on the eve of one of their most sacred holidays, a day marking the beginning of the long winter, a day when the veil between the worlds was the thinnest?

She prayed silently to herself that he hadn't heard her, and if he had, that he wouldn't alert her father to her presence. Her heart raced. Her nerves were a knot of worry. She wanted desperately to watch the ceremony but was terrified that the giant pirate would inform her father that she'd snuck out of her room and was spying on them.

That's when the shouts began, soon followed by screaming. Samhain was a time of celebration and occasionally bawdy behavior with little cause for terror. She risked peeking into the throne room and soon wished she hadn't. The giant pirate brought a long, curved, jagged silver blade to her father's neck. Her father's eyes met hers, and he whispered something just as the blade sliced his throat.

Blood spurted from the wound, covering the giant pirate.

"No!" she screamed.

She watched paralyzed as the giant strode to the wall she stood behind. She managed to back away, but not before she heard him roar, "She's in the tunnels. Find the princess. She's my prize!"

"As you wish, my Lord Balor," his men shouted, and hundreds of heavy boots thundered out of the throne room.

Tears ran down her cheeks. She wanted to curl up in a ball and cry for her father, but not yet. Not if she wanted to live.

She couldn't return to her rooms. That would only lead to imprisonment, and she would not be a slave. Not to the giant pirate. Not to anyone.

As she ran from the throne room, her face pinched and

her vision blurred, but it wasn't from tears. It was from something else. Something that felt an awful lot like magic. Had her father cast a spell on her as Balor slit his throat? She wanted to weep for the man who'd used his last breath to save her rather than to save himself. He was a noble faerie king, and she was nothing more than a spoiled princess who had snuck out of her chambers just so she wouldn't miss the festivities.

Soon her feet splashed in water. She must have reached one of drains that carried the castle wastes into the lake. How long before Balor's men descended upon her? Had they found other entries into the tunnels? Were they already searching the grounds? It was only a matter of time before she was caught, but she couldn't give up. She owed her father that much.

Her arms and legs ached with exertion—and something else. Her body seemed to be shrinking in on itself. But time was running out. She couldn't stop and figure out what was happening to her. Not with a giant pirate after her. She shook her head in anger. And to think she'd been worried about monsters in the dungeons—they were nothing compared to the one searching for her.

The water level rose until soon she was wading through it. It hindered her progress, but she refused to slow down. Goosebumps erupted across her skin followed by sharp pains, as if a thousand needles had suddenly punctured her flesh. She shrieked as she fought through the waist-high water.

Feathers poked out of her pores. She didn't understand what was happening.

Her arms and legs tucked up inside her body, shifting into wings and claws. An incredible pressure beat through her brain and exploded out of her nose—or what was once her nose. Now it seemed as if she had a beak.

"What's—" but before she could finish the thought, her body shot through the water like an arrow through the sky. No longer was she slowed by clumsy appendages like arms and legs. Now she swam through the water faster than she had ever moved before. She didn't know what her father had shifted her into, but she knew she was no longer completely human.

She dove out of the tunnel and plunged into the lake behind the castle. If she reached the surface too close to the castle walls, Balor might find her. She propelled herself through the water, pushing her new form to even greater speeds. When her lungs could no longer hold out, she broke the surface and took a deep breath. But it was no breath at all. It was a squawk, soon accompanied by other squawks. A cacophony of them. She found herself in the middle of a flock of . . . a flock of swans.

She'd never known a shapeshifter before. Had her father been one, or did he turn her into one to protect her?

A loud roar broke through the night. "Find her!" A man made that noise, but really not a man at all. Balor—part giant, part pirate, and part . . . something else. She didn't plan to stick around long enough to find out what.

A bright flash followed by a loud explosion erupted from the castle. Fire ignited the trees and brush that surrounded the castle walls, spreading across the countryside. Balor was going to burn down the world to find her.

And she refused to be his prisoner.

She was no longer the princess of the faerie king. She was Caer, orphaned shapeshifter who would be hunted to the end of the world. She didn't know where she would go, but she couldn't remain here.

Caer lifted her head, and her body followed. She flapped her wings and flew through the night sky. One hundred fifty swans followed behind her. They would protect her with their lives, just as her father had done.

To keep reading, grab your copy of SHADOW MOON: THE GODDESS CHRONICLES BOOK 4

REVIEWS ARE LIKE DANCE PARTIES. SOMEONE HAS TO GET THEM STARTED!

Keep reading for a sample of THRONE OF SILVER: SILVER FAE BOOK 1

THRONE OF SILVER: SILVER FAE BOOK 1

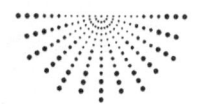

CHAPTER ONE

*D*ive in.

  That was the advice the swim team captain gave me when I gingerly dipped my toe in the pool at my first 5:30 a.m. swim practice three years ago. You see, the cold shocks your body into action. Stroke after stroke, you concentrate on your breathing, and the angle of your arms as they reach and pull through the water, and the height and depth of your kick, rather than on the freezing temperatures —at least that's the idea anyway.

Dive in.

I took that advice to heart. Made it my life's mantra, really.

So, when Sami texted me about a summer fellowship at Trevnor University's Leadership Academy, I begged her to pick me up an application. I couldn't think of a better way to spend June, July, and August than adding Summer Fellowship to my Georgetown application. My early acceptance was all but guaranteed.

But the entrance exam was tomorrow, at the tail end of

my post-season training for States, and in the midst of planning prom, Spring Fling, and our junior class trip, plus track started Monday.

Dive in.

My mantra sometimes got me in over my head.

CHAPTER TWO

*L*aughter exploded around me as I hurried through the school's front entrance. Over by the water fountain, four seniors played Hacky Sack while an audience of giggly underclassmen watched, making noises accentuated with rounded oohs and angled aahs. They all probably went to last night's basketball game too—the lucky bastards. While I discussed table linens and canapés with hotel managers, they got to watch the Webster Titans trounce the Bay Cardinals, 90-40.

Sometimes I hated these classmates of mine.

I mean *really* hated them.

None of them had two hours of swim practice this morning. None of them had two meetings during school, another meeting after school, followed by two more hours of swim practice. None of them had a To Do list so complicated and involved, even I knew it wouldn't be completed until after graduation.

Sometimes I wondered what it would be like not to worry about tomorrow, or next week, or next year. To live in the moment and just *be*.

A long stream of water hit me square on the nose.

Or not...

Shocked gasps ping-ponged through the ten-foot wide, locker-lined hallway, followed by an awkward, collective silence.

My body flickered—it had been doing that a lot lately especially when I got mad or annoyed about something. It felt like ocean waves slamming against my chest, and no matter how strong a swimmer I was, sometimes the big ones knocked me on my ass even when I was only knee deep.

I took a few deep breaths to calm myself. Thankfully, the flickering stopped. I was never standing in front of a mirror when it happened so I didn't know if the flickering was something other people saw or it was just in my head— which concerned me on a number of levels, but I couldn't worry about any of that right now. Someone needed to be punished for their crime.

I tracked the gaze of the surprised onlookers. My assailant, an underclassman with an unsteady grip on a green squirt gun, shook in his red Nike sneakers. I wiped my face and flicked the water in his direction. The droplets soared through the air and landed on his flushed, round cheeks. To his credit, he took it like a man, but unfortunately for him, he became the target of the dark, foul mood that descended upon me the moment I stepped into school.

"Don't you have a place you need to be?"

"Y...yes, sssorry Starrrr," he said, adding an overflowing consonant stream in the already crowded hallway. I narrowed my eyes. He tossed the squirt gun into the garbage can and sprinted away, red Nikes and all. When the plastic toy landed at the bottom of the can, it was as if someone hit play and all the students returned to their regularly non-scheduled lives.

Yep, today, I *definitely* hated them.

I stomped through the crowds, throwing the occasional elbow and the well-directed shove, because evidently, I was still the only one who needed to be somewhere.

Frank's buzzed head towered over the sea of students. I caught a glimpse of tight red ringlets by his side and understood why he didn't wait for me after practice.

He glanced down the crowded hall. A broad smile crossed his face the moment he saw me. One icy vein thawed. "Hey Starr," he said, then winked at the redhead. "I'll see *you* later."

"Bye Frankie," she replied, smiling like she just won the boyfriend sweepstakes. Frank was the total package—tall, dark, handsome with the brains and personality to match, but he wouldn't date Little Red long enough for her to find out. He went through girls faster than he swam the fifty, and he held the school record in that.

I frowned at him. "Frankie?"

He shrugged.

I spun my combination into my locker. "She already has a nickname for you?"

He smirked.

I tried my combo again, but my locker refused to cooperate. It was like it wanted to add further insult to injury.

At least in this case, I could cause bodily harm to it without being frowned upon. I kicked the base of the locker since my foul mood hadn't completely lifted and kicking metal seemed like a productive means to releasing frustration. Plus I didn't know what was up with the whole body flickering thing. I wasn't even sure if I wanted to mention it to my best friend.

Frank rested his hands on my shoulders and guided me to the side. He hit the locker just below the locking mechanism, and it popped open. He smiled as he rested against the locker next to mine. "When you got it, you got it."

I rolled my eyes.

"You know, I'm considered quite a prince to every girl in this school but..." He zeroed in a finger on my nose.

I swatted it away. "I know how charming you can be. The entire female population of Roger G. Webster High knows how charming you can be."

He closed the distance between us. "I can't help it if girls find me irresistible, but my dating days would come to an end if you went out with me."

Most girls would love the attention Frank gave me. *Most* girls would grow red-faced and faint if they heard half the come-ons he practiced on me. *Most* girls haven't been best friends with him since he was a short, obnoxious, hormone-ridden, scrawny seventh grader who wore ratty yellow Sponge Bob t-shirts and couldn't get a date to save his life.

I shoved him into class. "Get a grip."

To keep reading, grab your copy of Throne of Silver: Silver Fae Book One